I0781200

INCUBUS

COVEN: BOOK 12

DAVID NETH

DN Publishing

Incubus

Coven, Book 12

Copyright © 2024 by David Neth

Batavia, NY

www.DavidNethBooks.com

ISBN: 978-1-963602-17-3
First Edition

Subscribe to the author's newsletter for updates and exclusive content:
DavidNethBooks.com/Newsletter

Follow the author at:
www.facebook.com/DavidNethBooks
www.instagram.com/dnpublishing
patreon.com/DNPublishing

Also by David Neth

<u>**Lost By Magic**</u>
Lost By Magic
Lucky By Magic
Lured By Magic

<u>**Coven**</u>
Harpy
Siren
Valkyrie
Shapeshifter
Sorcerer
Witch (Short Story)
Enchantress
Oracle
Trickster
Poltergeist
Hex (Short Story)
Witch Hunter
Demon (Short Story)
Necromancer
Psychic (Short Story)
Incubus
Spirit (Short Story)
Human
Krampus (Short Story)
The Fates

<u>**Under the Moon**</u>
The Full Moon
The Harvest Moon
The Blood Moon
The Crescent Moon
The Blue Moon

The Art of Magic

<u>**Under the Moon: Villains**</u>
Toxanna (Short Story)
The Queen (Short Story)
The Dark Knight (Short Story)

<u>**Fuse**</u>
Origin
Omertá
Oblivion

<u>**Heat**</u>
Black Magnet
Dust Storm
The Gatekeeper

<u>**Standalone**</u>
All I Ever Wanted

CHAPTER 1

- JULY 1990 -

Orias lay back on his bed, lined with red satin sheets while one of his succubi fed him grapes. Another succubus was at his feet, massaging them with her hands. A third stood by and cooed at him, pointing her pouty lips in his direction and giggling whenever he smiled at her.

Rusalka entered his chambers with a stricken look on her face.

"Hello, my darling," Orias said in greeting. "It's so nice to see you. What seems to be upsetting you?"

She held back tears. Out of all the succubi in Orias's harem, Rusalka was the youngest.

"I have failed you," she said.

Orias waved away the other succubi who had been fawning

over him and sat up. "What do you mean, my dear?"

"You have sent me to find a man who would help me make a child. I did as you asked. I found a mate, I seduced him to have sex with me, but I'm afraid there isn't a child inside me. I know that for certain."

Orias stood and approached Rusalka. He placed a hand on her stomach and closed his eyes, sensing for life in her womb.

When he opened his eyes, he announced, "It's true. She is barren."

There were collective gasps from around the room. Each of the succubi stared at each other with worry and curiosity. Each of the demons in the harem had given birth to a child—or several—within their lifetimes. Many of the children had been traded for protection, or taken for the seductive powers they would eventually possess—whether they were incubi or succubi.

"Listen to me," Orias said to his ladies. "Our coven is growing older. Rusalka was the last succubus to produce another child to ensure the longevity of our coven. Without her child, we are facing an uncertain future."

The worried murmurs throughout the room increased. Without children to trade for protection—or to take care of them as they aged further—the coven would surely die off if all of the succubi could no longer produce children.

"Unless," Orias spoke up again, "we do something about this."

"But what are we going to do?" Rusalka asked. "I was the last hope."

"While it's true that the fertility in all of you has reached the end of its limit, my own fertility has no end," he announced. "As the only incubus in our coven, it is my duty to protect you all. And, if by providing that protection, that means leaving you all momentarily so that *I* can find a mate to provide us a child, then so be it."

More gasps filled the room, followed by protests. None of the succubi liked the idea of their incubus being with anyone other than someone from their coven.

"I know this is not the ideal solution, but it is our only choice to secure the future of our line," Orias said. "We will survive!"

CHAPTER 2

- WEDNESDAY -

Samantha rolled her eyes as her husband grumbled on the other end of the couch. She knew his thoughts on coming to see Dr. Bradford, but she didn't care. Their marriage was in trouble and so far, all of their attempts to reconcile weren't working.

"Good morning," Dr. Bradford said in greeting. "It's nice to meet both of you. I'm glad you decided to come and see me today."

Steven scoffed. "I bet."

She swatted at him. "Would you cut it out?"

He shrugged. "Sorry, but I just don't see why I needed to take the day off for this."

"Are you saying that you don't think your marriage is

important enough to take time off of work?" Dr. Bradford asked.

"Not, that's not what I'm saying," Steven said. "I just think that what's going on between a man and his wife should *stay* between a man and his wife."

"Except, we've tried that approach and it's still not working," Samantha countered. "Can you honestly sit there and tell me you've been happy lately?"

He crossed his arms and looked around at the books lining Dr. Bradford's office.

"Exactly!"

Dr. Bradford took a deep breath in order to quiet the bickering couple. "Why don't we start by identifying what the two of you view to be the problem in your marriage?"

"There isn't a problem—"

"He's been so distant and—"

"She's been so wrapped up in thinking that—"

"We *don't* talk, we just argue—"

Dr. Bradford held up his hand to stop them. "Why don't we try one at a time?" He pointed to Steven. "Why don't you start?"

"Honestly? I don't think we even need to be here. Samantha's the one who is so hyper-focused on destroying our marriage since our son was born. We were doing fine until all-of-a-sudden, I'm not doing *this* right and why'd I have to do it *that* way and I should just *know* what she expects from me. It's like, all of a sudden, she's determined to find fault with me."

Samantha's eyes grew wide. "I resent that! Yes, I may be more critical since Josh has been born, but that's only because I realize that we have an impressionable child watching us and seeing the examples we set for what a good person is and what a good marriage is. Honestly, I think we can both do better, but apparently *I'm* the only one who cares."

"Samantha, let's try to refrain from accusations," Dr. Bradford put in. "However, I do think it's a fair point to adjust your *attitudes* when you bring a child into the world. Naturally, as humans, our perceptions change. The child's needs come first a lot of the time, but that doesn't mean we can neglect other needs as well, such as the needs of our spouse. Now, before we move on, Samantha, is there anything else you'd like to share about what *you* think the trouble with your marriage is—again, let's try to keep the accusations to a minimum."

She let out a deep breath and crossed her arms as well. "I just get frustrated when I seem to be the only one—a lot of the times—who is working on our marriage. I'm the one who is worried about how I'm treating Steven or what I say to him and trying to find ways for us to spend time together away from Josh, but also find ways for us to spend time together as a family of three. And all of this on top of running the household and going to work."

Dr. Bradford nodded and turned to Steven. "Do you wish to offer a rebuttal? You said you think your marriage is doing okay. What do you think about Samantha's concerns?"

Steven shrugged. "I guess things *did* used to be easier between us, but we also just had a baby. There's an adjustment period. We'll figure it out."

The room fell into silence as Dr. Bradford studied the two of them. "When was the last time the two of you had sex?"

Samantha and Steven both stared at him in disbelief. Samantha felt a bit exposed for the shift in conversation to be such an intimate part of their lives.

"Has it been so long that neither of you can recall the last time?" he asked. "I know it's an uncomfortable question, but also a very important one."

"Well…" Steven started, then turned to Samantha to finish.

She nodded slowly. "We've…done it several times since Josh was born."

"And did you both enjoy it?"

Samantha crossed her legs and turned to look at her husband to take this next uncomfortable question.

Steven didn't say anything.

"I think the two of you need to readjust your thinking on your marriage," Dr. Bradford suggested. "Typically, when we're young and start dating, we're still living with family and so our partners are our escape from the world. Romantic dates are times for us to relax and unwind. We often don't notice that when we get married, things begin to shift. We initially think, 'Ah, this is great! I get to spend all of my time with this person.' And then the children come." He smiled widely. "And that's when we return to the idea of family and escapism. Not only is your partner someone you're sharing a family with, but they need to continue to be your escape from the responsibilities of the world. *Date* each other again, as if you were teenagers. And never stop."

"So…that's it?" Steven asked. "Your suggestion, at $100 an hour, is to go on a date?"

Samantha smacked his leg and furrowed her brow at him.

Dr. Bradford smiled. "Yes, for now. You need to reconnect with one another. *Talk* to each other. Enjoy each other's company. Connect intimately again so that you refuel the drive and the passion between you. That will make being partners in life so much more easier."

"So you're saying, just like, go to dinner or something?" Samantha asked.

"Go to dinner, go for a long walk, see a movie, whatever it is that the two of you enjoy doing together, do it," the doctor explained. "Find joy in each other's company again. Do you think that's manageable?"

Both Steven and Samantha nodded.

"Good," Dr. Bradford said with a smile. "Then that's your homework. Go on a date—or several—and try to reconnect…*intimately*. If you can do that, and prioritize each other again, you'll rediscover the importance of communicating with one another. It won't happen immediately, but little-by-little, you'll start to see improvements in your lives. Understood?"

Again, both of them nodded.

"Good. I'll see you again on Monday."

CHAPTER 3

The library was one of Kathy's favorite places, ever. She loved walking between the stacks of books, being surrounded by the possibilities of a million different stories, words, turns of phrases. Not only that, but the historic library brought her comfort with it's tall ceilings, intricate moulding details, and dark wooden panels. She loved the idea of so many people co-existing in a space, and yet having it be quiet enough to be able to focus and reflect on a million different thoughts.

At the moment, Kathy was perusing books on editing and writing. It was a skillset that she wanted to be able to expand on, considering that she didn't have very many marketable skills for employers.

She reached up to put a book back on the shelf, but as she

did the book pushed back another book that slid too far back on the shelf before she could catch it. It pushed into the books on the opposite side of the metal shelf and knocked those books back onto the floor in the next aisle.

"Whoa!" a man shouted on the other side.

Kathy rushed around the stack and saw several books scattered on the floor around a man who was rubbing his head. "I'm *so* sorry! I was putting a book back and it pushed the other ones back—are you okay?" She knelt down and began to pick up the books that had fallen.

"No harm done." He knelt down next to her to help. "Although, I have to admit that I never expected to be attacked in the library."

She rose to her feet, balancing books in her hands, and laughed at his joke.

The two of them locked eyes and Kathy forced herself to look away.

"So…architecture, huh?" She turned and started resolving the books. Idly, she wondered if it would be better to just take them to the checkout desk and explain what had happened so a librarian could make sure they were put away properly.

"Yes, it's an interest of mine." He handed her the books as she shelved them.

"Are you an architect?" She made sure the books were all neatly arranged on the shelf and in order according to the Dewey Decimal System.

"Unfortunately, no," he said. "But I've always been a fan of design. I have to admit that I'm not very artistic, myself. I'm much more of a numbers person, but art has always intrigued me. Perhaps it's because it's out of my skillset."

"I can understand that. You have an appreciation for it because you know how difficult it is."

"That's a nice way of putting it." He smiled at her.

Now that the books were put away, she had nothing to distract herself with. She searched for a polite way to exit, but couldn't come up with one.

"Are you an artist?" he asked. "Or creative in any way."

Kathy choked out a nervous laugh. "An artist? *No*. But I love reading…and I've always wanted to write a book." She shrugged. "I just haven't committed myself to sitting down and writing one yet."

"You should." He chuckled. "Trust me, at my age, you understand how short life really is and how quickly you'll grow to regret things."

"How old *are* you?" The question fell out of her mouth before she could stop herself. As soon as she heard it, her eyes grew wide and she clamped a hand over her mouth. "I'm sorry! I shouldn't have asked that!"

He laughed. "No, it's okay. I'm not offended. I'm fifty-two."

"*Fifty-two*?" Again, the words left her mouth without consulting with her brain first. "Sorry. I'm just surprised. You don't look that old."

Suddenly shy, he smiled and looked at the books on the shelf. "Well, thank you for that."

As she studied him, though, she finally saw the salt-and-pepper in his beard and the sides of his head, she saw the wrinkles near his eyes and around his mouth, and when he looked in her eyes again, she saw the wisdom that came with age.

"I'm twenty-three." It was her way of cutting off whatever interest was bubbling between them. They had both been flirting, that was for sure, but an almost thirty-year age gap was too much. They had no future together.

And yet, Kathy still felt the attraction between them.

He extended his hand. "I'm Charles Parrish, but I'd like you to call me Charlie."

She took his hand. "Nice to meet you, Charlie. I'm Kathy."

After they shook, he maintained his grip on her hand. "I need to get going, but I just wanted to thank you for not officially killing me today."

Her eyes fluttered to the books, then back to him as she smiled. "Yeah, sorry again about that."

"Maybe we can not kill each other again sometime." He pulled his hand back.

"Maybe."

"It was nice meeting you, Kathy." He began to walk backward, down the aisle. "Take care."

She waved and watched him walk away.

CHAPTER 4

- WEDNESDAY -

Steven pulled up the car to a stoplight. He and Samantha hadn't spoken since they had left counseling. The radio quietly played in the background, but neither of them were really listening to it.

"So," Samantha started, "where do you think we should go on our date?"

Steven, who was already annoyed at the car in front of him going too slow, simply shrugged. "I don't know."

"That's not a lot to go off of."

The light turned green and Steven quickly shifted into the next lane to pass the slow car in front of them, whipping back into the previous lane once he got around the other driver.

Samantha gripped the handlebar and braced herself against

the dash with her other arm. "Steven, slow down!"

"I was trying to pass that guy. He was pissing me off!"

Even though they had only been married a year, Samantha knew that the offensive driver was only a scapegoat for his annoyance. With his driving returning to a normal speed, she let the topic slide for a moment and they fell into another silence.

As he made another turn in the direction of Josh's daycare, she tried a different approach. "I want you to put an honest effort into this."

"Into what?" His tone was sharp, but still she pressed on.

"Our marriage. I want it to work. I want it to be a source of strength for us. Not a source of anger or resentment. I want Josh to admire it, and any of future kids that we might have."

Finally, Steven sighed. "Yeah. Me too. Why don't we go see a movie then?"

Samantha shook her head. "We won't be able to talk to each other during a movie. Maybe if we go to dinner or something beforehand—or, I know, we can go away this weekend. Yeah, Kathy can watch Josh and you and I can go to the Poconos or—"

"Sam, do you think we're made of money?" he snapped.

"Well, no, of course not." She had a part in handling their family's finances, so she was well aware of how much they had and it was enough for a one-night stay on the other side of the state. "I just thought—"

"I'm trying to put away money into an investment account for Josh."

That surprised her. It was something the two of them had talked about when she was first pregnant, but the idea hadn't been brought up again since. She liked the idea, and her heart warmed at the thought of Steven taking care of their son well into his future, but the fact that he hadn't discussed it with Samantha beforehand irked her.

"I can't do that if you keep spending my money," he said.

"*Your* money? Oh, that's right. Blame your wife for spending your money as if I don't have money of my own to use." She resented being downgraded to an overused stereotype. "For your information, I was planning on paying back the money for this trip from *my* funds. But right now I don't want to go anywhere with you."

"You don't have that kind of money."

She turned on him. "I have ten grand saved up in my own personal account. After my dad left and Kathy and I almost lost the house, I learned pretty quick to build up emergency expenses. And how much do *you* have saved up for emergencies?"

Steven gripped the steering wheel tighter in his fist.

"Yeah. That's what I thought."

They turned into the parking lot for Josh's daycare. Samantha unhooked her seatbelt and reached for the door to get out, but turned and looked back at her husband.

"I'm worried that if we keep going down the road we're going, we're going to end up divorced."

CHAPTER 5

- THURSDAY -

"I can't remember," Shirley said the next morning at work. "What else do I need from this patient?"

Kathy slid her chair over beside Shirley and, through a forced polite smile, said, "We need name, contact information, the medical notification form filled out, the HIPAA form, and insurance information."

Shirley still looked confused, but she sorted through the papers in her hand that the newest patient had handed her and finally said, "Okay. I think you're all set!"

The patient—a young blonde woman with her hair pulled back and her purse slung over her shoulder—smiled and said, "Thank you," before finding a seat in the waiting room.

Kathy closed the partition door and turned to Shirley. "Do

you know how to file all of that properly?" It was a question she didn't think she'd still be asking three months into Shirley's employment, but the woman had not caught on yet. Judging from the basic questions she continued to ask, Kathy didn't think she ever would.

"I think so. It all goes in the patient's file in the green filing cabinet?"

"First you need to enter it into the computer," Kathy explained. "It's a new system that Dr. Newberg is trying because we're running out of room for filing cabinets back here."

One of the things on Kathy's to-do list at work was to sort out the files of patients who had left the practice, moved away, or had died, to clear up space for new patients. But the idea of digging through six different filing cabinets top-to-bottom overwhelmed her. She could ask Shirley to do it, but she was afraid the woman would overlook something and throw out a file that they still needed.

"How can we help you?" Shirley's voice pulled Kathy's attention back to the front. Who she saw standing on the other side of the glass surprised her.

"Charlie! Hi!" Kathy blurted. Instantly, a smile spread across her face.

He returned the smile. "Kathy, how are you?"

She nodded. "I'm doing okay. There aren't any books here, so I think you're safe."

Charlie laughed. Humor looked good on everyone, but

especially Charlie. "That's good to know. I'm actually here for a teeth cleaning."

Kathy looked down at the patient list. Sure enough, the next one on her list was Charles Parrish. She didn't know how she had missed it when she first looked it over that morning. "Has your insurance or dental history changed at all?"

"Nope."

"All right, then you should be all set. You can take a seat until they call you back."

Kathy waited for him to turn away so that she could close the glass partition, but he lingered.

"I enjoyed meeting you yesterday," he said. "I was hoping I'd run into you again, but I didn't think it'd be so soon and I certainly didn't think it would be at the dentist."

She looked down bashfully. "Yeah, well, this is where I work."

"And you seem perfectly suited for it," he said. "You're friendly, approachable, and you seem to know your stuff."

"Thank you, but this is just where I am for now. In the future I hope to—"

"Charles Parrish!" the dental hygienist called out from the door leading to the patient nooks were.

"That's me," he said. "I'll see you on the way out?"

Kathy smiled. "I'm here until five!"

After he left, she closed the glass and then put her head down on the desk. Event hough she knew there was nothing wrong with being a receptionist, it was certainly not where she wanted to be in life. And to have Charlie, someone who was so poised, so well put-together, and so sure of who he was, see her in this intermediary part of her life was a bit mortifying.

"Was that your father?" Shirley asked quietly.

Kathy picked up her head and looked at her coworker. Two things hit her at once: the first was that Shirley clearly was not listening to the full conversation between the two of them that indicated she and Charlie were just acquaintances; and the second was that Charlie *was* old enough to be her father. In fact, he was *older* than her father.

What was she doing having a crush on a much older man? There was no future between the two of them. The crush would have to remain just that: a crush. Nothing good would come of her getting involved with someone so much older.

"Nope." Kathy shuffled the papers around on her desk to busy herself. "Not my dad."

Luckily, another patient approached and gave Kathy the perfect distraction to avoid further questioning from Shirley.

Twenty minutes later, Charlie returned to the front desk to check out.

"Looks like your co-pay today is fifteen dollars," Kathy told him. Better to keep her tone all business. There was a good chance that she would never see him again and she wanted to send the message clearly to him that she wasn't interested.

Charlie pulled out his wallet and fished for the bills in the large pocket. "I'm not really sure if you're seeing anyone, but I'd love to go out with you sometime. There's a place down on State Street that I'd love to take you to. Maybe have a drink, have some dinner, and do some shopping on State Street."

Her eyebrows raised as she took the cash from him. "A date?"

He picked up on her tone. "I apologize if that's too forward. If you're not interested in a date, then maybe we'll bump into each other again tomorrow at the library. Say, around five thirty? Then maybe—if you're interested—we could walk down to that restaurant I'm thinking of. Or, if you'd rather, you could knock more books on me."

That made her smile. "Okay. Maybe I'll see you there."

CHAPTER 6

- THURSDAY -

Samantha watched as Josh slept softly on his back in the crib. She gently ran the back of her hand down his sweet, round face before returning to her bedroom.

Steven was sitting up in bed, reading the newspaper like he did every night. He wore a plain white T-shirt and his watch still on his wrist. She had no idea how he was able to sleep with it on every night, but somehow he managed.

She tried to climb into bed without saying a word, but before she could turn away from him, he said the two words that broke through her barrier.

"I'm sorry." He folded the newspaper up and tossed it on the floor beside the bed.

Samantha turned to face him. "About?"

"For being grumpy with you this afternoon," he elaborated. "I just felt kind of…*exposed* after therapy because I really don't think we need it."

"I think the fact that we argued right after therapy and haven't talked since kind of shows that we *do* need it."

Steven reached out and ran a finger up and down her arm. "I know. And I'm sorry for that too." He leaned down and kissed her shoulder.

She pushed him away. "I'm not in the mood, Steven. I'm still kind of mad at you."

"But Dr. Bradford said that we need to make time for sex to build our intimacy."

Funny how he was against therapy until it led to the possibility of more sex. But still, Samantha agreed that she felt closer to Steven after they did have sex. And they weren't going to improve their relationship by holding grudges. If Steven was in a place to try to work on their marriage, then she needed to meet him halfway.

Giving in, she leaned in and kissed him and, with her eyes closed, felt him shift until he was hovering over her. She slid down her pillow, still kissing him.

Steven moved down to kiss her neck and she felt herself starting to get into it.

"You know," he said between kisses, "if we can get back into a routine of having sex, then maybe we can stop seeing the therapist altogether."

Samantha pulled back, which was hard to do when she lay flat against the mattress. "More sex isn't necessarily the goal of seeing Dr. Bradford. Sex and time together isn't just some checkbox to do every week."

"I didn't mean it like that."

"You better not have."

"I'm sorry. I didn't mean to ruin the mood." He leaned down and began kissing her neck again.

Samantha looked over his shoulder up at the ceiling. Her mind was racing. Her anger was growing. How could Steven be so obtuse to think that she only wanted more sex from him? Didn't he want the relationship they had had? The one where they enjoyed each other's company, found support in one another, and could tell each other everything to. That's what made the intimate part of their relationship so rewarding. That they could be completely vulnerable with the other person and still be accepted and loved.

Somewhere along the line, those priorities had changed for Steven and she was not about to go through the motions until he understood what they were trying to achieve through therapy.

Pressing her hands against his chest, she pushed him back as she sat up straighter in bed. "Never mind. I'm not in the mood anymore."

He sat back on his heels, his hands resting on her legs. "Seriously?"

She nodded. "Seriously. We need to reconnect through conversation before we can reconnect through sex. Remember what it was like when we were dating? We *talked* to each other. We made each other a priority. Just because we're married doesn't mean we can take each other for granted."

Steven let out a heavy sigh and looked back to his spot on the bed. "So…what? You're just never going to have sex with me again?"

She rolled her eyes. "Don't be so dramatic. Of course I will. But we need to work on some stuff before just right back into it. We need to start dating each other again."

Steven ran a hand through his hair, leaving it standing up on end. "Okay. Okay." He nodded slightly, then went back to his side of the bed, lay down facing away from her, and turned out the light. "Consider this as me *not* walking you to the door then." He pulled up the covers to his shoulder and kept his back to her.

Again, she rolled her eyes. If he was going to petty like that, then there was no talking to him. She lay down on her side of the bed and turned out the light as well.

But as the darkness surrounded them and they both pretended to fall asleep, all Samantha could think about was how good his lips felt on hers. They needed to work out what was going on between them so that they could get back to that.

CHAPTER 7

- FRIDAY -

Orias sat in one of the comfortable leather chairs against the wall in the library. He had a view of the front door, but he was tucked away in a corner so as not to seem too expectant.

As he sat, a beautiful woman took the seat on the opposite side of the end table beside him. He didn't glance in her direction, but kept his eyes firmly locked on the entrance.

"What are you doing here, Rusalka?"

She pretended to look through her purse. "Have you selected a mate?"

"I'm working on it." He shifted, resting his right foot on his left knee. "She will be here any moment and I can't have you around ruining it."

Rusalka nodded, finally looking at him, even though he still didn't turn to look at her. "I'll leave. I just wanted to let you know that the girls and I…well, we're worried that if you don't find a mate soon and spawn the next generation, then word will spread that our coven is dying and we'll be picked off."

"Listen to me. I am very much aware of the gravity of our situation," Orias said. "My first duty is to protect my harem. In order to do that, I need to find a mate who will be able to carry my child. As I've said, that is something I am actively working on."

"I don't mean to disrespect you," she said. "It's just that, typically, the girls and I are the ones in this world, finding mates and bringing home children. You're…out of practice."

"My skills at seduction are just fine," he said. "I may work differently than you—slower, perhaps—but rest assured, I will bring home an heir." Finally, he turned to look at her. "Now, I believe you know where the exit is. I don't want my future mate to be spooked off by another woman."

Both of them turned their attention to the main entrance, where a beautiful young woman stepped through. She had her brown hair pulled up in a bun and a bag slung over her shoulder. She lifted her sunglasses up on the top of her head and looked around.

"That's her, isn't it?" Rusalka asked.

"Yes, it is. Now go."

"She's beautiful." She looked over at Orias. "You've selected a good one." She got up and started toward the door, bypassing Kathy closer than Orias would've liked.

Naturally, Kathy smiled at Rusalka, offering innocent politeness to a complete stranger. That naïveté made Orias smile. He had selected a good one.

CHAPTER 8

- FRIDAY -

Kathy waved at Charlie when she saw him sitting in one of the leather chairs. He wore a button-up white collared shirt and a blue tie. The sleeves were folded up perfectly, revealing muscular forearms. As she crossed the space, he rose and greeted her with his own smile.

"Fancy meeting you here," she said with a laugh.

"Total coincidence," he said with a smile. "I'm glad you came."

"Honestly, I wasn't going to when you first asked me." She adjusted the strap of her bag on her shoulder. "But then I figured, why not? What else was I going to do on a Friday night? Stay home and read the books I picked up from the library a couple days ago? I wasn't feeling that today."

Charlie looked up, as if something just occurred to him. "Oh, you know what? I actually picked up some books from the library the other day as well." He shrugged. "I guess I have some time before I need to check out some more."

Kathy chuckled. "Three weeks!"

He nodded toward the windows. "I see the sun is still shining. What do you say the two of us take a walk on this beautiful day?"

That made her clam up. It wasn't that she didn't like Charlie. In fact, that was the problem. She liked him a little too much. But the comment Shirley made about him being her father still weighed heavy on Kathy's mind. What was she really doing with him?

But then, she had already turned him down to dinner, and she had showed up to the library like he offered. An innocent walk wouldn't mean anything more than just two people who enjoy each other's company enjoying the weather together.

"I promise, we'll stick to State Street or some other major roadway so there will be plenty of witnesses and opportunities for you to leave if you feel uncomfortable."

She shook her head. "No, it's not that. I just think…" She was trying to find a good way to tell him that there would never be anything between them. That their nearly thirty-year age difference was too big of a deal for her. But when she looked him in the eyes, she couldn't help but melt at his kind face, his handsome smile, and the intelligent mind that she knew he possessed.

"I enjoy your company, Kathy," he said. "It doesn't need to be anything more than that."

That made her smile. Even more, it made her feel safe. Heard. Understood. "Thank you. Honestly, there's something about you that I feel drawn to. It'd be a shame to ignore that."

"That it would." He offered his elbow to her and gestured to the door with his free hand. "Shall we?"

Kathy hooked her hand in the crook of his arm and followed him out into the waning sunshine.

CHAPTER 9

- Friday -

"How many?" the hostess asked when Samantha and Steven arrived at the restaurant.

"Uh, two…and a half, I guess." Samantha smiled at the girl as Steven carried Josh in his carrier behind her. "If you have a high chair, that should work for him."

The hostess smiled and waved at the baby, then grabbed a high chair from behind the host stand. "Right this way." She led them to a table, where they took a minute or two to get situated in their seats.

As the married couple looked over the menu, Steven murmured, "I don't know why we couldn't have dropped Josh off at my mom's for an hour or two."

Kathy had said that she had plans, which left them without

their usual babysitter.

"I told you, she's always so…weird around Josh," Samantha said. "Like she doesn't want to be around him for a long period or something."

"I think that's in your head. She loves him."

"No, she loves the *idea* of him," Samantha corrected. "Whenever it's convenient for her to play the 'Grandma' card around her friends or anyone else she's trying to impress. But when it comes to actually being Grandma, she's not interested."

"That's awfully harsh, don't you think?"

"Think about it, Steven. How many times has she stopped over to see him? Or called to ask how he's doing?"

"She's seen him often."

"Once a month since he's been born—at most. Hell, Kathy can hardly go three *days* without seeing him!"

Steven gave her a look. "Kathy is a little *too* attached."

"Oh, so now you're criticizing *my* family?"

"Well, considering how *your* mother nearly passed him off to a demon, I think it's safe to say that my mother will be getting 'Grandmother of the Year' for the rest of her life."

Samantha sat back and stared at him. "How *dare* you—"

"Can I start you off with something to drink?" the waitress asked when she approached.

Both Samantha and Steven grasped to find an answer for her in the midst of their argument.

"Um…I'll just have a coke, if you have it," Samantha said.

"And I'll just have water," Steven said.

"Of course," the waitress said. "Are we ready to order or do we need a minute?"

The couple exchanged looks before Steven turned back to her. "We need some more time."

After she left, both of them buried their noses in their menus.

"At least my father is good with him," Steven said, breaking the silence.

"Well, you father goes along with whatever your mother wants, and I don't want to put our six-month-old son in a situation where he isn't wanted."

"Again, that's awfully harsh considering—"

Josh threw the toy that he had been gnawing at across the table, then whined and reached for it.

Samantha handed it back to him and shushed him. "It's okay, Josh. Here you go. Here's your toy. Are you hungry? We're going to eat soon." When she looked back at her husband, she said, "Your mother would get annoyed with stuff like that because it would inconvenience her."

"You say that as if she didn't raise me."

Samantha raised her eyebrows. "I know. She's still trying to."

"You know, not to be too obvious, but Josh is a baby. He's not going to remember who did or didn't watch him. We need to give my mother a chance. She might surprise you."

"Or she'll meet every one of my expectations for her—

which is set pretty low, I might add—and make me feel like a terrible mother for putting my kid through that."

"Fine. It doesn't even matter at this point. He's here with us now. Can we just eat and go home?"

Samantha turned back to her menu, not even really reading the words on the page. So much for their romantic evening out. She didn't want to blame Josh for the rift between her and Steven, but having him complicated things. While she would never wish she hadn't become a mother, she recognized that before when she and Steven had a disagreement, there weren't as many distractions preventing them from sorting it out.

Now, the evening she thought would be relaxing and a way for her and Steven to reunite, had become stressful and made her want to be anywhere else than across the table from the man that she loved.

CHAPTER 10

- FRIDAY -

Kathy hadn't been paying attention. The conversation with Charlie came so easily that time seemed to pass by so quickly. He was a very intelligent man—well read and experienced in all different walks of life, yet also humble and kind and gentle.

Charlie said he'd always felt like a black sheep, different from those around him and someone who never wanted to be confined to a nine-to-five job, so he found other ways to make money and establish himself in the world. Kathy felt the same exact way about her life and talking with Charlie gave her hope that her life would turn out well after all.

She was so enraptured by their conversation that it came as a surprise to her when they came upon the waterfront. The feel of the cool breeze on her face was refreshing.

"Oh! I didn't realize we'd made it all the way down here," she said.

"Is that okay?"

She stared blankly, taking in the boats at the Presque Isle Yacht Club, and the lighthouse at the end of the pier. There were several boats out in Presque Isle Bay, the occupants enjoying the early evening sunshine.

"Kathy?"

"Hmm?" Her head snapped up to him. "Yeah, this is fine." Her stomach grumbled loudly and she reached for it. "Actually, I'm getting hungry so I should probably head home."

Charlie smiled and held out his hands for hers. "I have a surprise for you. Follow me."

Without question, she took his hands and let him lead her toward the marina. As they made their way onto the dock, Kathy found herself looking at Charlie with a new perspective.

He stopped alongside one of the boats and stepped on, turning back to reach for her hands. "Watch your step."

She let him pull her onboard and looked around. "This is *yours*?"

He smiled and nodded. "Yes, ma'am."

"Sorry if this is too forward but what exactly do you *do* for a living to afford a *yacht*?"

Charlie looked around and shrugged. "The word 'yacht'

makes it sound so…exclusive. This is a small yacht. Really a large motor boat."

She looked around, eyebrows raised. "This is still a yacht, Charlie."

He seemed to take it in through her eyes for the first time. "Yeah, I guess it is the biggest one in the marina."

Kathy took a deep breath, readjusted her purse on her shoulder and tried to look as if this didn't shock her any longer. "You never answered my question. What do you do for a living? Because whatever it it, I'd like to do the same thing."

He laughed. "I could help with that. I've been fortunate enough in my life to have made some very good investments and now, at this stage in my life, I simply spend my time managing those investments and spend the rest of my time…" He paused and rubbed his chin as he searched for the right word. "Enjoying life to the fullest."

"I'll say." She stepped to the edge of the boat and peered around to take in the full size of it. "If I'd have known I was coming aboard a yacht I would've dressed better."

"I think you look beautiful just the way you are."

The compliment ignited a fire inside Kathy that made her heart race. What was this man *doing* to her?

"But if you think you'd like to change, you're welcome to check out my ex-wife's closet down in the cabin." Charlie started for the stairs, but stopped when he didn't hear Kathy follow him.

"Wait a minute. You were *married* before?" Again, Kathy wasn't sure why that fact bothered her. Everyone came with a past—she had dated many guys, and at one point she thought she was going to spend the rest of her life with Jeremy until *that* blew up in her face. Why should Charlie be any exception? He was older—much older—so he had lived a full life. Maybe it was because the guys that Kathy typically dated were barely old enough to have a full time job, let alone get married.

What was she thinking, though? Charlie could be her *father*, as Shirley so delicately pointed out. There was no future for them. She was certainly *not* dating Charlie in any way, shape, or form.

"Yes, I was married before," Charlie said. "Does that bother you?"

In fact, it did. The jealousy had come on suddenly and completely. But she didn't want Charlie to know that. "Um…no, it doesn't. That's fine. I just think—I mean, don't *you* think that it'd be weird if I wore your ex's clothes?"

He shook his head. "Not at all. What I find a bit weird is a grown man owning all of these beautiful dresses and jewelry that he's *never* going to fit into. That's what's weird."

And just like that, he found a way to break through her barrier and make her smile. The jealousy started to melt away.

"Just take a look," he encouraged. "If you don't like any of it, you don't have to keep it. If there's something you see that you *do* like, feel free to take it."

"Are you sure?"

He reached for her hand and kissed the back of it. "I'm very sure."

He took her on a tour of the yacht, showing her the galley, the helm, and ending in the stateroom. Each room was small, but so elegantly furnished, even for a boat. The galley was well-stocked with food and the dishes were held in place so they didn't move when at sea, but everything looked purposeful. The aft deck was spacious and sunny, with lots of available seating. The stateroom was small, with barely enough room to stand in since the bed took up most of the space, but there were two closets on either side of the doorway leading to the stateroom.

"It's a relatively small closet," Charlie warned. "So I apologize if I had built it up to be more than it actually is."

"This is beautiful," Kathy said. "I can't believe you own this."

He opened the closet to the right. "Feel free to take whatever you like."

Kathy's eyes widened as she saw the space crammed with beautiful clothing. Gowns and sundresses and blouses and numerous swimsuits of all types. She pulled out the drawers at the bottom of the closet and saw all the jewelry. Rings and earrings and necklaces and bracelets.

"Your ex-wife didn't want any of this?" She ran her hands along the fabric of some of the clothes.

"She was more concerned about the contents of our house," he explained. "I think she forgot about these clothes, to be honest. And then in the divorce, I got the yacht, so I also got all of its contents."

"Still, you'd think she'd ask for it back when she realized she had left it behind," she said. "Especially because, as you said, you'll never wear it—at least, I hope not." She turned to see his reaction.

He smiled. "No, I have no interest in wearing any of that. Actually, I'd rather see you in some of it."

Kathy tensed up, suddenly realizing that they were essentially alone in his private bedroom.

"You said you were hungry?"

She nodded, suddenly feeling very close to him.

"I've arranged for a delicious meal to be delivered here. I'd love for you to join me because I'd hate to eat alone."

Kathy thought about her own choices for dinner. Leftover spaghetti in the fridge that she'd have to reheat in the microwave.

"It's your choice," he said. "I'll be upstairs waiting for the delivery man. Feel free to put on one of those dresses. Like I said, I'd love to see you in them."

After he left the room, closing the door behind him, Kathy looked back at the bed and suddenly felt a twinge of desire to fall back on it with Charlie. Instead, though, she clutched one of the dresses to her and wondered if she should wear it. She didn't want to end up being a carbon copy replacement of his ex-wife—they had strangely been the same size—but at the same time, she wanted to look nice for Charlie.

CHAPTER 11

Kathy felt a little out of place wearing another woman's dress. But that momentarily left her mind when she found herself back on the main deck and saw that the sky had turned to a beautiful red color as the sun set over the lake. Charlie had also plugged in the patio lights that were strung around the deck, giving a warm glow to illuminate the space.

"Wow," she said. "This is beautiful."

He walked up to her, looking particularly sexy in the setting sun. "Not nearly as beautiful as you."

She twirled to show off the dress she had chosen. It was a simple pink dress that helped show off her tan. She had pulled her hair back into a tight bun behind her head, to try to have some measure of elegance to her ensemble, despite the limited resources she had to work with.

"That dress looks fantastic on you."

Kathy smiled and thanked him, while simultaneously wondering if he had bought the dress for his ex-wife, and if she had worn it to impress him, just as Kathy was doing. Was Kathy just a replacement for his ex? Was she helping him fulfill some mid-life crisis?

The fact that he was old enough to be her father sprung to her mind again.

"Please, have a seat." Charlie held the chair out for her.

That's when she just noticed that the table had been covered with a white tablecloth and was adorned with beautiful dishes. In the middle of the table sat a metal platter with a matching lid, to help keep the food warm.

"Charlie, I'm impressed," she said after she was seated.

He stepped over to his seat and slid up to the table. "You are? My dear, this is all nothing. Just you wait."

She smirked. She loved being wined and dined. It was nice to be treated so royally. She almost felt like she didn't deserve any of it, and she shoved aside the idea that she owed him something for his generosity.

Not that Charlie expected anything more than she was willing to give him.

"The yacht, the dress, the food, the lights…" She shook her head. "It's like you transformed this whole place in the fifteen minutes that I was downstairs."

He waved it off as he reached for the bottle of wine chilling in the bucket of ice beside the platter. "It was nothing. The food was delivered. The dishes have been on board since I bought the boat, and the sun was a very happy coincidence. Wine?"

She considered his offer and tried to read the label, but couldn't make out what it was. With her budget, most of her wine consumption was driven by the price of the bottle. The cheaper it was, the better it tasted.

And that was certainly *not* Charlie's taste.

"Um…just a little."

He filled her glass until she raised her hand, signaling that that was enough. Then she lifted the glass, sniffed the wine, and took a sip. It was dry, but not overwhelmingly so. Fruity, but not too sweet. A perfect blend.

Almost like Charlie.

"Wow, that's delicious."

"I've had it aging for the last five years, waiting for the perfect moment to pull it out."

"And this is the perfect moment?" she asked.

"I'm here with a beautiful woman, watching a gorgeous sunset, and enjoying a delicious meal. What more could I ask for?"

She smiled.

Charlie lifted the lid off the platter and dished out the salmon and vegetables that had been delivered. Kathy had been trying to incorporate more fish into her diet, so she was happy to see what was offered, and when she raised the first bite to her lips and felt the savory flavor in her mouth she was surprised at how good it was.

"This is definitely delicious!" she said.

"Yeah? Do you like it?"

"I love it!" She swallowed the next bite, then said, "Charlie, this is all so…so…" She struggled to find the right word. Too much? A bit, but she also figured that Charlie wasn't one for small gestures. "This is all so amazing. I've had a great night with you."

"The night's not over yet."

She reached for her wine and took a sip. "Well, I've enjoyed your company so far."

"And I've enjoyed yours as well. You're a special person, Kathy. And so I want to treat you special. Just as you should be treated."

No other man that she had been with had made such a bold claim. Then again, Charlie was much older—and much more *mature*—than a lot of the other guys she had dated. This was a nice change.

"All I can say is, a girl can get used to this."

"I hope you do."

The spent the rest of the evening in easy chatter. Charlie casually mentioned that he had taken his yacht around Lake Erie, and even out to the Atlantic Ocean, where he spent a summer traveling up and down the East Coast.

After the sun had set, Charlie put on music and the two of them danced slowly on the main deck until Kathy could no longer ignore the chill of the night air. Even though Charlie insisted that she keep the dress, she changed back into her clothes, went back to reality, and thanked him for a wonderful evening with a hug and a promise to see him again, then meandered the marina until she found her way back to the bus stop.

CHAPTER 12

Samantha stared up at the ceiling in the early morning light that trickled through the windows. She heard her husband breathing heavy beside her, but she could tell from his breaths that he wasn't deeply asleep any longer. It was just a slow Saturday morning—one of the few they had now that Josh was mostly sleeping through the night. Some mornings he slept in late, others he was up at the crack of dawn.

What woke Samantha up wasn't the sun or the cry of her child, but the regret that consumed her as she thought about her and Steven's failed date the night before. Instead of bringing them closer together like they had intended, it had caused further tension between them. If they were going to move forward, she needed to put her pride aside, own up to the part she played in the disastrous date, and move on.

Looking over at Steven again, she reached out and shook his arm. "Hey, are you awake?"

"Hmm?" he grumbled.

She was right. He hadn't been sleeping. She leaned toward him so their faces were inches apart. "I'm sorry for last night. I hate arguing with you, especially since we were supposed to have a nice night out."

He squinted his eyes as he looked at her, then reached out and pulled her body closer to his. "It's okay. I'm sorry too. I wasn't in the best mood yesterday anyway and bringing Josh with us just…"

She nodded. "I know. It was an added stress that we needed to escape from."

"I love you." The morning breath was intense, but Samantha figured hers probably didn't smell much better.

"I love you too." She leaned in and kissed him.

They lay wrapped in each other's arms for a moment before Samantha rolled back to glance at the clock beside her bed.

"It's six-thirty. We probably have some time before Josh wakes up," she said. "Maybe we can make up for last night."

Steven opened his eyes fully, a smile spreading across his face. "Oh? I like that idea." He kissed her, then shifted his weight so that he hovered over her.

Samantha felt him on top of her and leaned into his kisses. Thankfully, Josh was sleeping in. That and early morning sex was a decent way to start the day. Especially since the night before had been such a disaster.

Steven moved down and began kissing her neck and she fished through the tangled sheets to find the bottom of his shirt and work her hands up under it and began caressing his back. Just as she hooked one of her legs around Steven's, the baby monitor came to life as Josh began crying.

Steven stopped kissing her neck and leaned his forehead against the pillow. Samantha's own body went slack, this time from annoyance and not arousal.

Nearly simultaneously, they let out a collective sigh, then both laughed.

"I guess this is what parenting is," Samantha said.

"I know he's only a baby, but he's a real buzzkill sometimes." Steven rolled back over to his side of the bed. "Are you getting him?"

"Yeah, I can." She tossed the covers back and sat up on the edge of the bed. She pressed her face into her hands and rubbed at them.

"Maybe when he goes down for a nap we can try again," he suggested.

"I was hoping to go grocery shopping when he's napping. It's so much faster if I go without him."

"Can't you go tomorrow?"

"I would, but we're running low on food. We're going to use the last of the coffee creamer this morning, and I'm going to need formula for Josh."

Steven sighed. "Okay."

She leaned across the bed and kissed him. "Why don't I call Kathy and see if she can babysit tonight? We can redo our date from last night and after we put Josh to bed tonight we can pick up where we left off this morning."

Josh relentlessly cried on the monitor.

Steven kissed her. "I'd like that."

CHAPTER 13

- SATURDAY -

"Ooo, I don't know, Sam." Kathy made a face as she held the phone to her ear.

"Just for a couple hours," Samantha pleaded on the other end.

Kathy took a deep breath and let it out slowly. Watching Josh for the evening would *seriously* ruin her dinner plans with Charlie.

At the same time, though, she missed Josh. She wished she could see him more than she did, especially now that she didn't live at the house with her sister. But she wasn't Josh's mother. She had her own life.

Samantha picked up on her hesitation. "Is there a problem?"

"I love Josh, and I'd be happy to take him anytime, but—I was planning on going on a date tonight."

"I didn't—you didn't say—oh." On the other end, Samantha let out her own sigh. "It's just that, Steven and I have been going through a bit of a rough patch lately and we tried to bring Josh on our date last night, but it didn't work out. Josh was whimpering and whining, and Steven was upset that I don't like his mother watching him. And then we had this argument, which is totally *not* the result we wanted after a date. We just really need a night out—just the two of us." She let out another heavy, exaggerated sigh. "But, I guess if you're busy, then we're the parents, not you. We're the ones who have to change our plans when we can't find a sitter. Josh will just have to go another day without seeing his Aunt Kathy."

Kathy groaned. Even the thought of disappointing that little boy crushed her heart. She knew Josh was too little to remember—or to truly care—but she did. And her sister knew that. "Oh, Sam, why do you need to put it like that?" She grumbled again. Charlie would understand. Besides, it wasn't like she was officially *dating* him. She just enjoyed his company, as Charlie had put it. "Okay. Fine. I'll watch him tonight. I guess I'll just call and reschedule my date."

"Thank you!" Samantha beamed on the other end. "And I know that I just completely manipulated you—"

"Mm-hmm, sure did."

"But Steven and I *really* need this night alone."

Kathy made a face as she studied the pattern on the backsplash tile in her kitchen. "Sam, I don't need the *details* of what you plan to do with your alone time with your husband. I think I can connect the dots myself."

"Sorry. But it's true. Steven and I need to reconnect. When you're married you'll understand."

Kathy thought back to her roller-coaster relationship with Jeremy. She thought she would spend the rest of her life with him. Now, here she was, over a year out from their most recent breakup and she was sure it was going to stick this time. "I understand just fine now. I'm just disappointed about my date."

"Yeah, let's back up for a second. Who is this new guy? You never mentioned him."

Kathy felt herself clamming up. She eyed the distance from the wall to the kitchen island stool and debated whether or not the phone cord would reach comfortably.

It was a distraction to keep from talking about Charlie. She knew that Samantha would take one look at him and note the age difference and immediately not like him. It wasn't like Kathy *needed* Samantha's approval of the man she was seeing, but she knew it would be nicer to have it if she did.

"Kathy?" Samantha pushed. "Who is he?"

"Well, I met him at the library."

"That's a good place to meet someone."

"We're still getting to know each other," Kathy said. "That's why I didn't say anything to you yet. I don't even know if I like him that much." That was a lie. She liked him a lot more than she should. And she had just met him. Why did she fall for guys so hard? Unless, like Milo, they were perfectly suitable for her and then she had to *force* herself to like them.

She wondered how Milo was doing since his own encounter with magic...

"You like him enough to be disappointed about missing a date with him."

Kathy crossed to the stool and sat. The cord pulled, but she wrapped it around her shoulder so it wasn't pulling on her ear. "That's true."

"So what's he like?"

"Sam..."

"What? I'm just asking! We used to exchange stories all the time about the guys we dated."

More like the guys *Kathy* dated. Samantha had had a couple boyfriends in high school, but when she went to college and met Steven, the two had basically been inseparable ever since.

"Give me some details!" Samantha pushed.

"All I'll say is that he's very much a gentleman. You'd like that about him."

"Well good. I'm glad that you finally found a nice guy. You deserve to be happy—and you deserve someone who treats you special."

CHAPTER 14

The candles were all lit throughout the house, casting each room in a sickly sweet scent that smelled to Orias of sex. It was one of the aphrodisiacs he used on his mates. Typically, those aromas, coupled with his powers of seduction and general charm, was enough to lead women right to the bedroom to fulfill his deed as an incubus.

Rusalka appeared in a puff of smoke. She made a revolted face at the candles and waved a hand in front of her nose. "Ugh! What smells so bad?"

"It's Kathy's favorite scent." Orias lit the last of the candles with the lighter. "Sandalwood with nutmeg and a hint of cinnamon and undertones of vanilla. This will help her feel warm and welcome to my home. This will help her feel as though she belongs her, which will allow her to lower her inhibitions and may even lead to her going to bed with me."

"Well, it smells horrible."

Orias turned on her. "It's not for you. As a succubus, you don't require aphrodisiacs. All that matters is that Kathy likes it."

Rusalka crossed her arms. "You think candles are going to make her want to have sex with you? I thought you understood women?"

"Are you questioning my leadership? My prowess? If so, when I'm successful and have planted my seed in Kathy's womb—and make no mistake, I *will* be successful—I do not have to continue to mate with you once I return to my true home in the underworld."

Rusalka took on a somber look and bowed her head. "My apologies, sir. I meant no disrespect. It's just that, the reason it's so easy for me and the other girls to find a mate is because human girls are more resistant to sex."

Orias shook his head. "They're not resistant. They're careful. Which is precisely why I need to make Kathy feel as comfortable as possible."

She nodded. "I understand now. So you believe that tonight is the tonight?"

"I'm going to try." He walked around his lakefront house, fussing with the decor, making sure each and everything was perfectly in place and aligned just so. He wanted Kathy to think he had casual elegance. Like his house looked like this at all occasions. He wanted her to have the impression of him—or rather, his Charlie persona—as someone who was intelligent. And intelligent people tended to have tidier homes. "I don't believe, as you've pointed out, that Kathy goes to bed that easily, though."

"Have you been using your seduction powers on her?" She sat on the brown leather couch, which shifted the carefully-placed throw blanket that lay over the back.

He shot her a look and fixed the blanket, opting to fold it and place it in a basket beside the fireplace. "Of course I have, but I have to do it slowly. She's a witch and I need to make sure not to tip her off to my true intentions. Otherwise, it could mean the end to our whole coven. So if you would stop interfering with my efforts to keep our line alive—"

"With all due respect, it's pretty risky, going after a witch."

"I know. I need to take the risk. Our coven is dying and we need to step up our game if we're going to repopulate." He crossed to the wall and straightened several of the picture frames that were hung in a group. Scenic views from throughout the world, portraying the image that Charlie had traveled all over on his yacht. "I hope that whatever offspring Kathy and I create is a succubus. This effort to impregnate poor unsuspecting women is beneath me. As you pointed out, it's much easier for a woman to take a man to bed for casual sex."

Rusalka nodded. "That it is. And it's much more fun for us."

The phone rang and Orias moved across the room to

answer it. "Hello, Parrish residence." How quickly he was able to slide back into his Charlie character.

"Charlie? It's Kathy."

He smiled. "Kathy! I was just thinking about you. I'm very much looking forward to seeing you tonight."

"Actually, about that, I need to reschedule," she said. "I'm so sorry."

He made a face of annoyance, but quickly recovered with a smile. Even though she couldn't see it, he needed to keep the chipper, happy tone to his voice and the smile would help with that. "Don't be. I hope that everything is okay."

"It is. I just got strong-armed into watching my nephew tonight."

"How old is he?" Orias rolled his eyes at how sickly-sweet his voice sounded.

"Six months."

"Perfect!"

"I'm sorry?"

"Bring him over," Orias said. "I can help you keep an eye on him. After he goes to sleep, the two of us can…chat."

There was silence on the other end. "I don't know…. Are you sure that's okay?"

"Of course it is! Not a problem at all. You're a wonderful person, and I'm sure you're a great aunt to your nephew. I'd love to get a glimpse of that."

"Okay." The relief in her voice was evident. "Then I guess

we'll both be over later. Thank you, Charlie!"

He put the phone back in its cradle and stared at it. The evening's plans had been altered, but not obliterated. He'd have to change tack. Instead of charming Kathy as a woman, he'd have to speak to her motherhood instincts. Maybe plant an image in her mind that she'd love to be a mother—a mother to *Charlie's* child.

"You're inviting someone else over while you try to bed the witch?" Rusalka asked. "I hardly think that's a productive way to get her to—"

"Not *someone*," he corrected. "Her nephew. A baby."

"Won't that prove as a distraction?" Rusalka asked.

Orias stepped to the fireplace and checked the mantle for dust. "No. By inviting her nephew, I'm making Kathy feel safe by showing her that I accept the child in her life—as well as her outside responsibilities. And by insisting she come over, I'm making her feel desired, which is what every woman wants."

CHAPTER 15

- SATURDAY -

"It's so nice to have a night away," Steven said as he lay the cloth napkin in his lap.

Samantha ran her finger along the rim of her water glass. "It is, although I do miss Josh."

"Sam, it's okay to have a night away from him once in a while," he said. "He's safe. He's with your sister. She wouldn't do anything to hurt him."

"I know. It's just a little bit of Mom Guilt. And I know that it's important for you and I to have time alone, just the two of us. I've been fighting for it for the last couple days."

"This is true." He reached for his water and raised it to his lips. "Do you think it'll be this hard when we have more kids?"

Samantha raised her eyebrows and studied her husband.

She tried to hold back the smirk on her lips. "Have you thought about us having more?"

He nodded once. "I have."

Still trying to show nonchalance, she asked, "How many do you want?"

"Well…we only have one other bedroom in the house, unless I can convince you to move out of this house and find another one that's larger."

Samantha shook her head. Her enthusiasm for the future of their family was getting the better of her. "That's not necessary. Multiple generations have lived in the house for years and years before we came along. We can manage with some more kids. Besides, depending on how many we end up having, we can put the boys in one room and the girls in another. If we really have to, we can start converting the attic or the basement into bedrooms—or maybe even build an addition!"

Steven laughed. "I think if we ever got to a point where we'd have to reconstruct our house to have more kids, then maybe we should *stop* having kids."

"You probably have a point. But you never answered my original question: how many kids would you like?"

He considered. "Maybe only one more, two at most. Although, to be completely transparent, your…*after work activities* make me nervous about having a houseful of kids."

Samantha's face dropped. She watched the condensation on her glass roll down to the white tablecloth. The "after work activities" that Steven was talking about was, of course, her responsibilities as a witch. Something that scared her for the safety of her son—and any future children—more and more every day.

"Well, I've kept Josh safe so far…"

"Sam. You were possessed when you were pregnant, and Josh was kidnapped by your dead mother a couple months ago."

"Oh." She adjusted her silverware on the table. "I didn't realize you were keeping score." Regret bubbled inside her. Was she a terrible mother? Did Steven think so? Was she being selfish by wanting to have children even though their lives were dangerous sometimes? What if something happened where she *couldn't* protect them? And if Josh had already been kidnapped once, did she even do a good enough job protecting him then? Had she already failed as a mother?

"I'm not keeping score," Steven assured her, "But I can't ignore that those things happened. And neither should you. I'm not worried about *you* protecting our kids. That fact is, *I* can't always protect our kids. Not in the way that you can. I just don't know if the constant stress and worry for them is worth filling the house with kids. Parents already have enough to worry about."

Samantha knew that her husband had a point. She knew that he was right. And she agreed with him. She just wished that things were different. Safer.

And she wished that the time alone together that they had finally got hadn't been spoiled by reminders of things outside of their control.

CHAPTER 16

- SATURDAY -

Kathy shushed Josh as she rocked him in her arms. They were aching from carrying him for the last half hour, especially as he snuggled into her chest, leaving her standing in an awkward position until he drifted off to sleep.

With his breathing remaining steady and light, Kathy knelt down to the baby carrier and slowly set him in. She hoped that he would stay asleep. If worse came to worst, she would freeze him long enough to work the kink out of her neck before she picked him up again. But she wanted to limit magic use around Charlie. It was bad enough she needed to bring a baby on her date.

Luckily, Josh only tilted his head to the side and continued sleeping.

Kathy closed her eyes in relief and then went back into the living room, where Charlie was waiting.

"Sorry about that." She reached for the glass of wine that she had placed on the coffee table. "But I think he's out for the night, so no more interruptions."

Charlie smiled. "Don't apologize. I like seeing you in a maternal role. You'd make a good mother someday."

As she sipped her wine, her eyebrows raised up. "*Someday.*"

"Do you want kids?"

Kathy settled into the couch as she thought. "I like the idea of a traditional family. I think having a husband and two kids sounds nice."

"But?"

She looked over at him with a tight grin. "But one thing I'm learning about myself is that I'm not really a traditional kind of girl, no matter how hard I try to make it work."

His brow furrowed. "What do you mean? In what way aren't you traditional?"

Like being a witch, she thought, but kept it to herself. "I guess my job. This is going to be a little embarrassing to admit, but it's the first real nine-to-five job that I've ever had, but I'm just not happy. Don't get me wrong, having the money to pay for things is a huge bonus—the steady paycheck makes things really easy."

"But?" he prompted again.

She smirked. "But every day when I go into work I feel like

I'm being someone that I'm not. Like who I am is being eroded away for the sake of making a living." She shook her head. "I don't like that. And I'm a little afraid that motherhood would make me feel the same way. The difference is, you can quit a job, but you can't take back being a mother."

Charlie reached over and took her hand, rubbing his thumb on top of it. "Oh, Kathy. First of all, let me tell you that anyone who's ever done anything extraordinary very likely feels the way that you do about having a steady job. There are just some people not cut out for a regular *nine-to-five*, as you put it. And there's nothing wrong with that. It just means you were meant to do bigger things that your struggles—and your free time—will allow you to achieve."

Kathy knew that this was certainly a pep talk, but she let him talk because, somehow, it was making her feel better. Validated.

"And second," he went on, "becoming a parent is an experience unlike any other. It's one that I'm certain you'll never regret."

She smiled. "You sound like you're talking from experience. Do you have kids?"

Charlie took in a deep breath and released it slowly. Kathy felt her heart race faster with each passing second. She knew the answer without him having to even say it. Yet again, their age gap was coming up as a reminder that this romance wouldn't work out.

"Would it bother you if I said yes?" he asked.

In a split second, Kathy wondered if she was cut out to be a step-parent. If her interest in having kids would be fulfilled by helping raise someone else's kids.

And then she was struck with another thought: what if Charlie's kids were her age? He *was* old enough to be her father. So instead of helping to raise his kids, she'd be mistaken for their sister.

"Of course it wouldn't bother me," she said with a forced smile. "I'd rather you were honest. If this…relationship is going to go anywhere, we need to be honest." At what point, exactly, did she consider the two of them to be in a relationship? *That* was a feeling that she did like.

"I don't want you to think differently of me."

Now she squeezed his hand. "I promise you I won't."

He nodded. "Then yes. I am a father."

"How many do you have?" It was the only question she could ask that was closest to the one she really wanted to ask: how old are they?

Charlie seemed to back off a bit. His eyes traveled up to the coffered ceiling as he debated how best to answer. "I have…a few."

She narrowed her eyes. "A *few*? Most of the time when people talk about their kids, they rattle off their names and ages like baseball stats."

"I have more than the average man," he admitted. "I told

you I didn't want you to think differently of me. Can we please change the subject?"

"Well, I'm curious," she said. "Can you at least tell me if you have boys or girls? Or if you're still in touch with their mother? Is that the ex-wife you mentioned?"

"Kathy, this will all come out in due time."

She set her glass down and shifted on the couch to face him as she took both of his hands in hers. "And I'm asking now. I think it's time."

"Mostly girls. And my ex *is* the mother of some of them, but some of my kids have other mothers as well."

Mothers. As in plural. As in multiple women he's had children with. As in multiple women he's slept with. As in multiple women he's dated. As in how many other women did he sway with his charm, just as he was doing to her?

Kathy had a hard time keeping her reaction from her face. Her shoulders hunched up and her hands slipped out of his.

Charlie sighed. "I knew you'd look at me differently if you knew."

"Having kids is one thing, but having a whole *soccer team* is another. Give me a minute to process this." Her mind was spinning as she wondered just how many kids he had, and just how many *women* he'd gotten pregnant. Was she about to become the next mother to his ever-growing list of children?

She felt herself growing sick and turned to set her feet on the floor and put her head in her hands.

Charlie shifted so he was sitting beside her. He rubbed his hand on her back. "Tell me what you're thinking so I can help you feel better about this."

"I'm thinking you're a serial dater," she blurted. "I'm trying really hard not to think of you as a guy who dates women, gets them pregnant, and then leaves them when the baby comes. Like some guy who gets off on getting a girl pregnant just to dump her because she got fat." She shook her head and felt the tears well up in her eyes. "Sorry. That was uncalled for. I just don't want to be the next girl on your list."

He moved over even closer so they were sitting side-by-side and pulled her onto his chest. "Oh Kathy. I don't know how to change your mind about me other than to say that with each of the women I've had children with, there was a genuine relationship. All of my children were born out of love. Each of my children were wanted." He rubbed her back. "I promise. I will take good care of you."

Kathy sat up and looked at him. She was torn between her intense desire for him and her mind alerting her to the red flags. But she followed her heart as she kissed him hard on the mouth, feeling sparks flutter in her stomach. Sparks she hadn't felt in a long time.

CHAPTER 17

"Kathy?" Samantha called as she stepped into her sister's apartment and turned on the lights. "We're here!" She glanced at the clock on the wall. Just after nine o'clock at night. Josh would definitely be asleep. She only hoped that Kathy had had the forethought to put him in pajamas and a clean diaper so that when Samantha took him home she could just put him right to bed without disturbing him too much.

Samantha was surprised that Kathy's apartment was empty. Not only because Kathy was supposed to be watching Josh, but because Samantha thought that she and Steven had been running late. After dinner, they had decided to go for a walk and enjoy the clear, warm, quiet summer night and indulge in further conversation.

Now that Samantha saw that nobody was home at Kathy's, she was regretting that walk.

"Where is she?" Steven asked.

"I don't know."

"Do you think something magical came—"

The door opened and Kathy walked through with Josh's carrier hooked in the crook of her arm and his diaper bag slung over her shoulder. "Oh, hello. Sorry for running late."

Samantha's eyes widened as she watched Kathy set Josh and his bag down on the kitchen island. "Where the hell were you? It's after nine!" She was relieved to see her son sleeping peacefully—in pajamas—in his carrier.

"I know, I had to cut my date a little short."

The older sister gritted her teeth and glared at her sister. It took everything in her to keep her anger in check for the moment. With her eyes locked on Kathy, Samantha said, "Steven, take Josh down to the car. I need to talk to my sister."

Without any hesitation, Steven slung the diaper bag over his shoulder, grabbed ahold of Josh's carrier, and stepped out of the apartment without further comment.

When they were alone, Samantha finally unleashed her annoyance. "Kathy, what the hell were you thinking? You *never* should've taken Josh out of the apartment without telling me where you were taking him! What if something had happened?"

"Nothing happened." Kathy moved to the cupboard and pulled out a cup and filled it with water at the sink.

"Where were you?"

"I told you. I had a date."

"You were supposed to cancel that."

Kathy drank some of her water. "I tried. Charlie suggested I bring Josh to his house so we could still have our date after Josh went to sleep, which we did. Josh did great."

"That's not the point." Samantha tucked her hair behind her ears and crossed her arms. "It didn't occur to you to let me know you were taking my baby to a stranger's house? That was reckless and stupid."

"You're being dramatic. Charlie is nice. He wouldn't hurt me and he certainly wouldn't hurt Josh. If anything, I thought it was more of a turn-on that he wasn't put-off by me having to babysit. It shows he has maturity."

"Kathy, you don't know anything about this Charlie guy. You've only known him a few days!"

"And I really like him!" She grinned. "Like, *really* like him."

Samantha let out a sigh. "That's great, but it still doesn't give you the right to take my baby to his house."

"Sam, I really don't think I did anything wrong, but I'm sorry I upset you," Kathy said. "I will ask you next time I want to do anything with Josh. But, let me point out, that I *told* you I already had plans and you twisted my arm into taking Josh so that *you* could go on a date. Why is it fair for you to have a date but not me? Last I checked, *you* were his mom. That means that *you* need to make the sacrifices and I don't."

Samantha bit her lip. Kathy had a point. A very good one. Samantha was in no position to throw stones. And yet, she was still mad at her sister.

So instead she changed tack. "What do you even know about Charlie?"

"I know enough about him to trust him."

"Like what?"

"Like…he owns a boat. He's had a lot of success with stocks and he's pretty loaded. His house on the lake was very nice and clean—and he didn't hesitate to baby-proof it before Josh came. I only had to take a couple things away from him when I was there."

Samantha narrowed her eyes. "So he's rich and he picks up after himself and *that* makes you think he's trustworthy with my baby?"

"Well, he has kids himself."

"He does?"

Kathy nodded. She busied herself with wiping some crumbs from the counter and pushed them into the sink.

"How many?"

"He…didn't say." The younger sister averted her eyes, fussing with some crumbs that were still left on the countertop.

Samantha rolled her eyes and started to turn to the door, but she stopped before she stepped outside. "Kathy, just be careful. You may have gotten lucky today with Josh. Don't let your loneliness get in the way of your better judgment."

CHAPTER 18

- SATURDAY -

Samantha sat up in bed with her arms crossed. Her eyes were locked on the wall across the room, but her mind was spinning with arguments she could've—and, perhaps, *should've*—made to Kathy. She also came up with reasons to justify her own manipulation of her sister, which, deep down, she knew was wrong. She shouldn't have persuaded Kathy into babysitting Josh if she already had plans, but it had never been a problem before. Why was this time any different?

Steven came back into the room and closed the door behind him. "Josh is passed out. I think he'll probably sleep straight through the night." He began unbuttoning his shirt and pulled it off.

"That's good." Samantha only casually looked over at him.

She wasn't mad at Steven, but she was still mad. And not in the mood to talk. Or sleep. Her mind was going a mile a minute.

Steven pulled off his undershirt and tossed it on the floor. "I had a good night with you."

"Me too." She chewed on her lip. When was Kathy going to learn? Samantha had thought that becoming an aunt had matured Kathy a little bit, but maybe not as much as Samantha had hoped.

Steven pulled off his pants and folded them before setting them on top of his dresser. He crawled into bed and climbed over Samantha's outstretched legs.

Maybe if Kathy had still lived with them, she would know just how much sacrifice it took to raise a child, Samantha wondered idly.

"What are you thinking about?" Steven leaned in and kissed Samantha's neck.

"That Kathy needs to grow up." Samantha wasn't paying much attention to her husband, although a part of her felt discomfort as his stumble grazed her neck.

"Forget about Kathy for right now. It's just you and me." His hand found its way under the covers and up her shirt.

"It's just that she should've *told* me that she was taking Josh to her boyfriend's house," Samantha went on. "Or had the boyfriend come to her apartment instead. *Or maybe* she should've introduced him to us so that we could feel better about the person our son was spending the evening with."

"Mm-hmm," Steven murmured against her neck. "She was wrong."

"It's stuff like that that makes me nervous about leaving the house at all without Josh."

"Honey, you're going to need to cut the cord eventually."

That snapped Samantha's attention right to him. "Excuse me?" She pushed away his wandering hand.

He leaned back on his heels. "Did you forget that *we* had plans tonight?"

"I'm not in the mood."

"You've been putting me off for several days now. *'Oh, tomorrow. Later. Not now.'* Well, later never comes." He fell back on his side of the bed and stared at the ceiling. "It's frustrating."

"Well, I'm sorry if I'm not turned on after our son spent all night at a stranger's house without us knowing!"

Steven sat up again and pointed toward Josh's room. "He was with your sister! He wasn't hurt. He's fine! He's sleeping right now, safe in his own room. Sure, Kathy should've told us, but she didn't. So can we build a bridge and get over it?"

"Maybe this is me getting over it," she countered. "Either way, I'm not in the mood to have sex right now."

He rolled his neck. "Look, I know you're upset, but if we're going to do what Dr. Bradford said in counseling, then we need to make time for each other."

"Oh, so *now* you're interested in what Dr. Bradford says? When there's the possibility of sex?"

"And what about you? You can't just pick and choose when you're concerned about our relationship. Either we need help or we don't. And if you're going to keep stringing me along like this, then maybe you need to rethink your commitment to our marriage."

Samantha stared at him slack-jawed. She was at a complete loss for words at his accusation, so she didn't say anything as he got out of bed, grabbed his bathrobe from the back of the door and left the room.

"Where are you going?" she asked.

"To sleep somewhere else," he grumbled. "I wouldn't want to bother you anymore than I already have."

Before Samantha could protest, he shut the door with a slam. She expected to hear Josh start crying but all she heard was silence.

CHAPTER 19

Kathy stepped out into the sunshine on Charlie's boat. Sunglasses were perched on her nose, shielding her eyes from the bright sun. In only a bikini, she felt the warmth on her skin and she breathed in the salty, cool ocean air.

She walked to the edge of the boat and felt the wind flow through her hair. She reached for her iced tea, which was in a tall glass on the ledge, and took a sip. Cool and refreshing.

Kathy had never felt more relaxed.

She heard footsteps behind her and she turned to see Charlie come up from belowdeck in his own swimsuit. She admired his muscles and the confidence in his walk.

He came up behind her and wrapped his arms around her, kissing her cheek from behind.

"Hello, my love. Are you happy?"

"I'm with you. Of course I am."

And she was. She felt at ease, safe, loved. She leaned back into his embrace as they looked out onto the waves.

It wasn't until she raised her hand to hold onto his arms that the light caught the diamond on her finger. She was Mrs. Parrish. Charlie's wife.

That thought alone made her swell with pride.

"Good." Charlie reached down and rubbed Kathy's belly. "Because the two of you make me the happiest man in the world."

Kathy placed her hand over his and felt the baby kick in her belly as her heart beamed with contentment. This was where she belonged.

Kathy shot up in bed. Her heart was racing and her body was sticky with sweat. She ran a hand through her hair, pulling it away from the sweat dripping down her forehead.

She groped at her belly and felt its flatness. She felt relief as the reality of her *not* being pregnant sunk in. Then she looked to her left hand and saw that there was no ring there, either.

It was just a dream.

And yet, she couldn't get the image of Charlie's near-naked body out of her head. Or the pleasure she got from knowing that she was his wife and had his baby growing inside her. It should've scared her. Becoming a wife and a mother wasn't something she thought about often. But, to her surprise, the prospect inspired her.

What was more, when she looked at the clock and saw that it was only two in the morning, she hated that she still had so many more hours before she could see him again. She wished he was in bed beside her, so that she could hold him. Lay her head on his chest and relax in his embrace.

Charlie Parrish had a hold on her, that was for sure. But that passion—that *need* to see someone—was intoxicating. It was a feeling that Kathy hadn't felt in a very long time.

And she was going to enjoy it.

CHAPTER 20

- SUNDAY -

Samantha rolled onto her side and felt the cold bedsheets beside her. She cracked her eyes open a little, squinting against the sunlight starting to creep through the cracks in the curtains.

She groaned when she saw Steven's side of the bed empty. Their fight the night before came rushing back to her. Instantly, she was filled with regret. Why did she have to harp on Kathy's misjudgment so much?

Steven was right. If Samantha wanted to work on their marriage, she needed to be willing to do the work. She had made a promise to Steven the night before and she had broken it.

Rolling over to her other side, she looked at the clock beside the bed. It read 8:03. Her eyes opened wider and she sat up.

Eight o'clock? She hadn't slept in this late since she had the baby.

Josh must've been tired, she thought to herself. She pulled the blankets off and stepped out into the hallway where she was surprised to see that Josh's bedroom door was open. A glance to her right showed that the door to Kathy's old bedroom was open too. The sheets on the daybed were ruffled too.

The thought of Steven sleeping in another bed made Samantha's heart sink. Wasn't one of the age-old marriage advice 'never go to bed angry'? Or had that been disproven?

Regardless, Samantha wanted to share her bed with Steven again and she made a promise to herself that she was going to make things right so that he would return.

Down in the kitchen, Steven sat at the table in his robe. He had a coffee mug in his hand and a box of Cheerios sat on the table in front of him. Josh sat in his high chair, his hands slicked with saliva and chewed-up Cheerios. He smiled happily at his mother when she walked in and raised his fists—clutched tight with more Cheerios—in celebration.

"Good morning." Samantha kissed the top of Josh's head. She studied Steven, but he kept his eyes on the back of the box of cereal. Apparently whatever was on the back was more interesting than greeting his wife in the morning.

But Samantha pushed that aside. She had promised herself that she was going to make things right.

"I made you coffee," he murmured.

"Thanks." She went over to the coffee pot and poured herself a cup. She added some creamer in and one spoonful of sugar, then carried the cup back to the table, where she sat beside Steven.

When she was seated, Steven looked over at her. "I'm sorry for getting mad at you last night."

She reached for his hand. "I'm sorry too. I ruined a perfect evening."

"No, I shouldn't have expected you to still be in the mood after your argument with Kathy. I shouldn't have pushed you."

She squeezed his hand. "Thanks. But you're right about what you said, though."

He sat up, surprised by her admission. "Oh?"

"We need to make our marriage a priority. Last night, I should've been focused on you instead of what *might've* happened to Josh. Like you said, he was home, he was safe, and I had made it clear to Kathy that she shouldn't have taken him without telling us." She shrugged. "We did all we could do. I should've enjoyed the time alone with you instead."

Steven brought her hand to his lips and kissed the back of it. "So where does that leave us now?"

"Well," she said with a smirk, "when Josh goes down for his nap, I'm all yours."

He smiled. "I can't wait."

CHAPTER 21

The sweat dripped from Kathy's forehead as she stepped back into her apartment. She knew that she smelled. A three mile jog in the middle of July would do that to you.

She had been running every day for nearly a year now. Not only was it a way for her to keep fit and clear her mind each morning, but now she had new motivation: to look as good as she could for Charlie.

This morning, however, she was also hoping that her jog would get her mind *off* of him and that vivid dream she had had of being his wife and carrying his baby. But, as she placed her headphones on the kitchen counter and stepped into the bathroom to take a shower, she realized the jog had done just the opposite. She couldn't seem to get Charlie out of her head.

In the shower, Kathy tried her hardest to think about anything else, but her thoughts kept coming back to him. How sweet he was. How smart he was. How much he wanted her in his life. How much she *wanted* to be in his life.

More so, she couldn't help but wonder if Charlie's body really did look like it did in her dream the night before. Was he really that lean; that muscular? Would his arms feels as good around her as they had in the dream?

Abruptly, she turned the water to icy cold. She needed to get a grip. Samantha was right. Kathy had no business being this infatuated with Charlie after only knowing him for a week. *Less* than a week!

But she wanted to be with him.

Kathy turned off the shower and reached for her towel. As she dried off, she heard the phone ringing. She tucked the towel around herself and hurried into the kitchen to catch it before it ended.

"Hello?"

"Kathy! It's Charlie."

She felt her whole body flush. "Oh, hi. I was just thinking about you."

"Oh yeah? Only good things, I hope."

Again, she felt her face flush and her body prickle with sweat. Maybe she would need another shower. "What's up?" Her attempt at sounding casual came out as awkwardly as she felt.

"I would like to know your address."

"It's 1313 State Street. Apartment A." She cringed, wondering if it was wise to throw out her address so easily. Then again, she had been to his house—with Josh, nonetheless. Hadn't she swore to Samantha the night before that Charlie was harmless?

But something else nagged at her. Charlie's house was expansive. Elegant. On the lake. Her apartment was quite the opposite. She looked around at the brick walls, the large windows with cobwebs up at the top where she couldn't reach, and her mismatched furniture that she had picked up at second-hand stores. If he came to her apartment, she wasn't sure she could survive the embarrassment. Yet another reminder of their age differences and places in life. Not to mention the difference in their wealth.

"What do you need my address for?" she asked.

"I want to take you shopping," he said. "You deserve your own nice dresses to wear, rather than wearing my ex-wife's clothes. You were right, it wasn't right of me to expect you to wear someone else's clothing."

Kathy shook her head and lifted her wet hair off the back of her neck. She was growing hot at the prospect of more attention from Charlie. She wanted him to want her—and he did—but the voice of reason inside her head, the one that at the moment sounded more like Samantha than her own voice, told her that she needed to cool it for a day or two with Charlie. Space was what she needed in order to regain her level head and see things clearly again.

And yet, the ache to see him was impossible to fight.

"You don't have to buy me anything."

"I know I don't have to," he admitted. "I want to. You're worth it. I want you to look—and feel—amazing when I take you out. You deserve to look your best. I want you to feel as beautiful as I see you."

Kathy bit her bottom lip in an effort to stifle her smile, but it didn't work. Charlie knew just what to say to make her feel special.

"Well, I think I'd be stupid to turn down an offer like that," she said. "But I just got out of the shower, so I'm going to need a little time to get ready."

He let out a soft moan on the other end. "Now there's something for the imagination."

Heat came over her whole body again as the prospect of Charlie seeing her naked filled her mind. And the thought of seeing Charlie naked, too. And how they would—

Get a grip, Kathy, she told herself.

"Are you still there?"

She cleared her throat. "Yeah. Give me an hour. Then I'll meet you down on the street."

"Good. I'm looking forward to it. It's a date."

CHAPTER 22

- SUNDAY -

Samantha and Steven finally had some time alone. The conditions were perfect. It was the middle of a Sunday, the errands had been run, Josh was asleep, and they had spent the morning making eyes at each other and smiling at each other and flirting with each other.

But as Samantha lay in bed, with her husband on top of her, and their hands wandered over each other's bodies as they kissed, her mind was on a million other things *besides* her husband.

For one, she really hoped that Josh was truly asleep. Steven had offered to put him down for his nap and, truth be told, Steven was in a rush to have alone time with his wife. In her experience, Josh sometimes needed to be held and rocked for a while before he finally gave in and went to sleep. The fact that Steven had put Josh down for a nap within fifteen minutes left her skeptical.

Then she started thinking about Kathy. How they both had had time to decompress from their argument the night before. Samantha had time to think about and reflect on her reaction. She still wasn't happy that Kathy had taken Josh to Charlie's without her permission, but what was done was done. Josh was safe and nothing bad had happened. It was just a nervous mother's precaution—but one that Kathy should've anticipated herself. Samantha figured that if the of them two met up for coffee or even hashed it out over the phone, within a few minutes they would resolve whatever bad feelings they had left over the night before's argument.

The truth was, Samantha missed her sister. Ever since she had moved out, they hadn't spent as much time together as they used to. Of course, Samantha knew that was normal, but it still didn't sit well with her. They used to be so close and now it felt like they were drifting apart. Maybe that was why Samantha had gotten so mad at Kathy for taking Josh to Charlie's. Samantha didn't know anything about him. She didn't know anything about Kathy's plans to see him. Normally Samantha knew, at the very least, the *basics* of the men in Kathy's life and when their dates were. Sure, that was mostly the result of living with her sister, but Samantha still missed it.

"I love you so much," Steven muttered against her lips.

That brought her back to the present moment. She needed to focus. She was supposed to be making love to her husband—not thinking about her son and her sister at a time like this.

"I love you too." She wrapped her arms around his neck and pulled him closer.

His kisses moved down to her neck.

Maybe this was all they needed. Time alone. Maybe she was overreacting about the troubles in her marriage too. Did they just need to have sex more often?

No, she knew it was more than that. She and Steven had been growing distant too. They used to be able to talk about anything. Now, it seemed like anytime the slightest disagreement came up they either fell into the silent treatment or they started arguing. The arguing *might've* been productive, except for the fact that they both usually said things they didn't mean, and when they said things they *did* mean, neither of them actually listened to the other.

Steven suddenly pulled away. "What's wrong?"

Samantha furrowed her brow. "Nothing's wrong." She reached for his neck to pull him back to her, but he resisted.

"No, I can tell that your mind is elsewhere."

She sighed and dropped her arms down to the bed. "I'm not really into it right now."

That emitted a heavy sigh from Steven as he pulled away from her and flopped onto his side of the bed.

"I want to be, though!" she added quickly. "I'm just…not."

He stared up at the ceiling and brought a hand to his forehead, then ran it through his hair. "It's fine."

She rolled onto her side to look at him. She felt bad that she was disappointing him. Despite this being the perfect opportunity, they still just weren't clicking. What were they doing wrong?

Her hand traced up and down his arm. "Why does it have to be so hard?"

He looked over and grinned at her. "That's not exactly the problem."

Samantha gave him a look.

His expression turned serious as he turned to face her too. "Well, having a baby changes things. Hell, *marriage* changes things. Honestly, we kind of rushed into the whole parenting thing right after we got married and we're just now coming up for air, so to speak."

"Yeah, I guess you're right." She rolled over and backed into him, wrapping his arms around her with her back pressed against him. "I just didn't think we'd have these problems, you know? We've always had a good relationship. I didn't think having a baby would've changed that."

He squeezed her in his arms and kissed her shoulder. "We'll figure it out. This is just a bump in the road. Growing pains."

"Promise?"

"Promise."

CHAPTER 23

- SUNDAY -

Kathy hadn't ever been happier. Not only because she was spending the day with Charlie—and he was buying her whatever she wanted—but she also got to shop at the clothing store she used to work at and flaunt Charlie's money in front of all of her old coworkers.

Of course, his money wasn't necessarily *her* accomplishment, but she wanted it to be known that someone so wealthy—and gorgeous—wanted to spend his money on her.

Kathy came out of the fitting room in yet another outfit and modeled it for Charlie.

He held up his hands and gave her a small applause. "Beautiful. Kathy, you're stunning."

She smiled and twirled for him before looking at herself in

the mirror. It was a short black dress that had cutouts on the side, revealing parts of her toned stomach.

"Are you sure we even need this one?" she asked. "You've already bought me six others."

"If you want it, I want you to have it."

"Well, if you insist." She turned and started to retreat back to the fitting room, but he caught her hand and pulled her to him, planting a big kiss on her lips.

"I want to see you wear that out on our next date."

She wiggled her eyebrows. "Well, first you need to ask me. And then I'll consider it."

Charlie bit his bottom lip and released her. Teasing, Kathy walked slowly back to the dressing room and turned to look over her shoulder at him before closing the door behind her.

As she unzipped the dress, she looked at the next thing hanging on the wall. It was a swimsuit—a bikini, just like the one she had been wearing in her dream. As soon as she saw it on the rack, she knew it was a sign. And with the universe telling her to take the swimsuit off the rack, she trusted that it was the right size too. If it didn't fit, the dream would never become a reality.

After dressing back into her regular clothes, she grabbed the pile of dresses—as well as the swimsuit—and draped them over her arm.

Charlie stood from the bench when she emerged. "All set?"

"In here, at least."

He nodded toward the register. "Let's go cash out, then."

The cashier seemed to recognize Kathy, but for the life of her, Kathy couldn't remember the girl's name. So instead, Kathy pretended like she was just another customer and *hadn't* been an employee of the store last year.

Maybe that was the reason Kathy had been getting dirty looks from the cashier as she bagged up her dresses and took Charlie's credit card. Or maybe it was the fact that Charlie was the one paying for all of Kathy's outfits. Either way, Kathy wrote it off as jealousy and once she had the bags in hand, she led Charlie out of the store and into the concourse of the mall.

"Is there anyplace else you'd like to stop?" Charlie asked when it was just the two of them.

Kathy eyed the lingerie store across the way, then turned back to him and smiled.

He put up his hands. "Let the record show, I'm not pressuring you to do anything you don't want to do."

She leaned up on her toes and kissed him. Just a peck at first, but as she felt his hands on her back, she leaned into the kiss.

When they finally parted, she said, "I want you, Charlie. And I want to look good for you."

Taking his hand, she led him into the store with a mischievous grin on her face.

CHAPTER 24

Kathy lay on top of Orias and kissed him passionately. She wrapped both arms around his neck and entangled her legs with his. In effect, she was pinning him down to the couch, but with her tongue in his mouth, there was no way for him to object—not that he would want to.

"Thank you," Kathy told him as she came up for air.

"For what?"

She pulled back enough to glance down at him. "What do you mean, 'for what?' For everything you bought me today! You spent a small fortune!"

Now it was his turn to pull her to him. He kissed her once, then said, "You're worth it."

She grinned and when she kissed him again, she played

with his bottom lip between her teeth.

As Orias let out a groan of pleasure, Kathy sat up.

His hands reached for her, finally settling on her butt. "Where are you going?"

She stumbled from her position on the couch and then retrieved one of the bags from where she had dumped them all on the floor after their shopping trip. In the air she raised a small pink one.

"There's something I've been dying to model for you."

Orias sat up on the couch with a smile. "Again, I just want it to be known that I'm not pushing you to do anything you don't want to do."

Kathy leaned over seductively, placing her hands on his knees so that they were face-to-face. "Don't you want me?"

He bit his bottom lip just before leaning forward and kissing her. "Of course I do."

She turned and carried the bag off into the bedroom, walking so that her lower half shook seductively.

Orias bit his bottom lip as he watched her walk away.

"Have you sealed the deal yet?"

He jumped at the sound of Rusalka's voice, and turned to see her suddenly sitting on the end of the couch. "How long have you been sitting there?"

"I just got here," she said. "So, have you bedded that witch yet?"

Orias stood and went to the credenza behind the couch,

where he fixed himself a drink from the crystal decanter. "I'm working on it. And I'll be much more successful if you weren't here to ruin it."

"The girls and I are getting worried," she said. "A hunting trip never usually takes this long."

He sipped his drink and looked out the back window onto Presque Isle Bay. "I told you. This is different. She's a witch. I need to move slowly so as not to raise suspicion. Rest assured, I'm moving as quickly as I can."

"Not fast enough."

Orias turned on her. "Let me remind you that our roles are different. As a succubus, you simply need to fool a man into having sex with you. That can be accomplished with some flirting at a bar. But as an incubus, I need to work a little harder to bed a woman. Especially a witch."

"Are you falling for her?"

"Don't be ridiculous. When have you ever known me to develop feelings for a vessel? No, my heart lies with my harem, which I will return to just as soon as I can be assured that my heir is on its way."

"Good. We miss you."

He extended his hand out for her. Rusalka took it and stood.

"You, and the other girls, are the only ones I'll ever need in my life." He kissed her softly on the lips. "This is just business. For us."

Rusalka sighed and nodded. "I know. I just don't like

spending so much time away from you. None of us do."

"I will return as soon as I can." He glanced over at the direction of the master bedroom. "Now go. Before the witch returns. If all goes well, I can return home in a few days—with the witch pregnant and as my prisoner, of course."

Rusalka turned toward the door.

"So, what do you think?" Kathy suddenly appeared in the entryway to the master bedroom, flaunting her new pink negligee. When she spotted Rusalka, her eyes widened and she covered herself with her hands before retreating to the bedroom.

"Kathy, wait!" Orias stepped toward her, ignoring Rusalka's departure. He stepped into the bedroom, where Kathy was pulling on a silk bathrobe—another new purchase.

"Who the hell was that?"

"She was—no one! She was no one!"

Kathy tied her bathrobe and then put her hands on her hips, eyebrows raised. "You're going to have to do better than that."

"She just stopped by to say hi. I told her I had company and she was just on her way out." He stepped toward her and tried to reach for her, but she put up her hand as a warning, her face still hard. "Kathy, come on. You're blowing this way out of proportion."

"What's. Her. Name?"

Orias hesitated, weighing his options. "It doesn't matter what her name is."

"Then there's no harm in telling me."

"Kathy, you're the only one that I want. Come on, we were going to make love for the first time tonight."

"We *were*. We're not anymore. Not ever, for that matter." She brushed by him and left the bedroom.

He turned and followed her. "Where are you going?"

She stepped into the kitchen and reached for the phone. "I'm calling my sister to come pick me up."

Orias tried to grab the phone from her, but she jerked away, giving him another hard look.

"Don't! If you ever want to see me again you'll let me go."

Breathing in a deep breath, he stepped back and put up his hands in surrender. "Okay. But you don't need to call your sister. Let me drive you home."

She held the phone to her ear as it rang. "I can't stand to be in the same room as you right now." Then she turned her attention to the receiver on the phone. "Sam? It's Kathy. I need you to pick me up, please—no, I'll explain when you get here. I'm at Charlie's house. We had a fight. I don't know the address. I'll be walking down South Shore Drive. Near Frontier Park."

"This is ridiculous, let me—"

She turned her back to him. "Thank you, Sam. I'll see you in a bit." After she hung up the phone, she moved around the kitchen island to put space between her and Orias.

He followed her as she made her way to the bedroom. "Kathy, let's talk about this while we wait for your sister."

"I can't talk to you right now. I need to think."

He cursed Rusalka for ruining this. He had Kathy in the palm of his hand, ready to let him bed her. Now he needed to play damage control and hope that she would forgive him—and soon—so that he could put a baby inside her. His coven depended on it.

"Kathy, I don't know what else to say other than I'm sorry—not that there's anything to be sorry about."

She whirled around on him as she began to repack her bag. "There's nothing to be sorry about? Are you kidding me?" She crossed her arms and planted her feet. "Okay. So tell me. Who was that woman and why was she here?"

"That was…she was…" No explanation that he could think of would put her mind at ease. He thought about saying that Rusalka was one of the mothers to one of his children—a fact that he didn't want to admit but that Kathy had taken surprisingly well—but he knew that would make Kathy uncomfortable. Like Rusalka—or any other mother—was still an active part in Charlie Parrish's life. If he was going to get Kathy to trust him, then she needed to feel secure and not threatened.

Unfortunately, the magical lust he'd been feeding her was now backfiring. The intense passion she felt for him was now turned into intense betrayal and hurt.

"Exactly." She glanced down at her bag. "You know what? This stuff can wait. I just need to get out of here." She eyed Orias, who stood in the door. Their eyes met for a moment before she darted to the bathroom.

For a fraction of a second, he considered reaching for her to stop her, but that would make her feel as though she were in danger. So he stood where he was and watched as she slammed the bathroom door shut.

After a few minutes, he opened the bathroom door and saw that the window was open and the screen had been popped out. Kathy was gone.

CHAPTER 25

Samantha spotted Kathy walking down South Shore Drive, barefoot and wearing a silk robe. And by the looks of it, not much else.

She honked lightly to get her attention, then pulled over on the side of the street.

When Kathy got in the car, Samantha's big sister instincts kicked it.

"What are thinking, walking around dressed like that? You could've gotten hurt! Anyone could've stopped and taken you, or taken *advantage* of you. Not to mention the fact that you're barefoot!"

Kathy burst into tears, which softened Samantha's tone.

As Samantha meandered through the city streets, she let

Kathy have a moment to herself. She knew Kathy was not in a position to hear a lecture just yet, and if Samantha opened her mouth that's all that would come out. The silence was better.

Samantha had been making dinner when Kathy had called and, as much as she didn't want to leave the house, things between her and Steven had been…awkward since their failed attempts in the bedroom. And with only Josh to distract them, Samantha welcomed the idea of shifting the attention off of her marriage for a bit and onto Kathy.

Not to mention, Samantha had been wanting to talk to Kathy all day. On the drive over, she had rehearsed an apology that would let her sister know that she was sorry for arguing, but not about her fear of what could've happened to Josh.

Kathy's tears had erased all of that, though.

"What happened?" Samantha asked quietly, once they were on West 6th Street, heading toward State Street.

"I think Charlie might be cheating on me."

"What makes you think that?"

"There was another woman there tonight and he refused to tell me who she was."

Samantha sighed. "Okay. But that doesn't mean he's cheating."

Kathy picked at her robe. "Open your eyes, Sam. What do you think was going to happen tonight?"

The older sister glanced over. Looked like she and her sister both had similar plans for the day. And it looked like those plans were ruined for both of them. She had reservations about Kathy's actions, but she pushed those aside. "But if he was about to sleep with you, why would he invite this other woman over? It doesn't make sense."

Kathy shrugged. "I don't know. Maybe she figured out we were together and wanted to stop something before it happened. Charlie and I were together all day at the mall. Anyone could've seen us."

"Maybe."

"He was married before," Kathy admitted. "And he has kids with several different women."

Samantha sucked in her lips to keep her comments to herself. The more she learned about Charlie, the less she liked him. But judging by Kathy's reaction, her sister was head-over-heels for him.

"I don't know. Maybe he hasn't moved on from them yet. I have a feeling he's had a kid with that woman."

"What makes you say that?"

Again, Kathy shrugged. "I don't know. Just a feeling."

Samantha pulled onto State Street. "Well, I think what's best is for you to put some space between the two of you for a bit. Give it a day or two and then see how you feel. Start with a conversation—over the phone. Then, depending on his answers, figure out how you want to proceed."

Kathy wiped her tears away. "I just feel like a complete idiot. Betrayed. I mean, I totally put myself out there tonight. I thought he was a good person."

"At the risk of sounding like the nagging older sister, let me just point that you've known him less than a week," Samantha said. "I'm sure there will be more surprises that come up. Maybe this is a sign that you should move slower from now on. Isn't that what you said you were going to do?"

Kathy was quiet as she thought about it. Then, "Yeah, maybe you're right."

Samantha noted that Kathy sidestepped her question about taking things slow with Charlie, but decided not to push it. Kathy had heard the words. The idea was planted.

They were quiet the rest of the way up State Street. When Samantha finally pulled over on the side of the street in front of Kathy's apartment building, she looked over at her sister.

"Do you want me to come up with you so we can talk?"

Kathy shook her head. "No, thanks. I just want to be alone right now."

Samantha nodded. "Okay. But call me tomorrow after work so we can talk about it some more."

"I will. Thanks, Sam." Kathy gave her sister a sad smile, then stepped out of the car and crossed the street to her building.

CHAPTER 26

- SUNDAY -

Orias slammed the bathroom door shut behind him and stormed out into the living room.

"Rusalka!" he barked out. "Get out here, *now*!"

From the foyer, she stepped out in front of him. She looked down at the floor timidly.

He set his hands on his hips and glared at her. "Well, she's gone. She saw you and got spooked off, just like I warned you about. Is there something you have to say for yourself?"

"I didn't think—"

The sound of Rusalka's voice—of the beginning of her excuse—enraged Orias. His hand shot out and he grabbed ahold of her throat. Both of her hands went up and tried to pry his off, but he held firm.

"I have half a mind to kill you right now."

Unable to speak, Rusalka stared at him with terrified eyes.

"Are you trying to sabotage the whole coven?" he asked.

"No," she croaked out.

He released his hold and turned to where he had set his drink the first time he had talked to Rusalka.

"I-I thought you, uh, that you had already bedded her," she stammered. "That your seed was inside her and you were just trying to convince her to come back with us. Make it seem like it's her choice, for the baby's sake."

"I told you, I need to take things slow with this one."

"Yes, sir."

Orias finished his drink as he watched the waves crash along the shore through the window. "This may be a good thing, though. This will serve as a test to my relationship with Kathy. Every couple fights. This will be her first instance where she questions her commitment to me. If I can prove to her that there isn't another woman and convince her to sleep with me, she will have complete trust in me. Her body will be relaxed and more likely to create a child with me—even if she's unaware."

"That sounds like a tall order."

He turned to look at Rusalka. "Yes, and as I told you before, bedding a woman as an incubus requires more skill and deception than it is for a succubus to take a man to bed."

She nodded.

"But only a few more days," he added. "I can already feel my own need to satisfy my sexual appetite reaching a breaking point."

This brought a smile to Rusalka's face. "How about I take care of that for you?" She stepped forward and gently placed her lips on his.

Orias returned the kiss, leaning into it deeper. Then abruptly, he pulled away. "No. If I want to ensure the witch's pregnancy, then I need to save my energy for her."

Rusalka pouted. "But it's been so long since you've been home. The girls and I miss you. We need you."

"And I will return to satisfy your needs just as soon as I've finished here," Orias promised. "Now, go report back to the girls. If they're so worried about how long I've been gone, I need you to reassure them that I'm putting my plan in motion and I will return to them as soon as possible."

She leaned in for another kiss. "Hurry home, sir."

"Of course, my dear."

CHAPTER 27

- MONDAY -

"So," Dr. Bradford said with a smile as he plopped down in his leather chair across from Samantha and Steven. The sound of the fabric rubbing against itself was loud as he sat, but everyone ignored it. "It's been almost a week since we last spoke. How have you been doing with the *homework* I assigned?"

Samantha looked over at her husband before she answered. "Well…we've gone on several dates, but…"

Dr. Bradford narrowed his eyes. "But…?"

"We haven't been able to, um…*finish the deed*, if you catch my drift," Steven said.

"It's not for lack of trying," Samantha added. "We've tried a couple different ways to rekindle the intimacy, but it's hard."

Dr. Bradford nodded. "That's normal. You have to expect delays and setbacks. You're not aligning with one another the same way you used to. You're out of sync. If reconnecting was as simple as heading back to the bedroom, you wouldn't be here talking to me. But the important thing is to make the effort. Take the steps to try to reconnect. Other than the bedroom, have you had intimate conversations with each other?"

Steven shifted uncomfortably on his end of the couch. "Like…fantasies and stuff?"

The doctor laughed. "Not quite. No, I meant more along the lines of your hopes and dreams. What you're most proud of having accomplished in your life. What you still hope to accomplish. Maybe reminisce about some of the fun times the two of you have shared together. Or maybe share a story that the other one has never heard before."

"We've started to," Samantha said. "But I think we can do a better job of it."

"Try focusing on the happy things," he said. "And keep trying. Listen, life happens. You have a son who demands a lot of your time and energy. You both have jobs. Life is hard and requires us to give a part of ourselves that we don't always have the energy for, right? That's why we end up fighting with our spouses—it's because at the end of the day when we get home, they're there and you feel safe with them to finally unwind from the day. We tend to take advantage of the people who've always been there and will always be there. And that can lead to tension and cracks in our relationship that could crumble if we're not careful."

Samantha glanced over at Steven again. It was as if Dr. Bradford knew exactly what was going on in their relationship. She knew that she took Steven for granted and she didn't want to anymore.

"You're two independent people who are constantly evolving and changing as life throws different curveballs at you," Dr. Bradford went on. "What we all need to do in order to keep our relationships from crumbling—to keep them in sync, as we've discussed—is to be vulnerable enough with the ones we love most to tell them when we've had a bad day. Allow them to comfort us and support us, and do your part in being comfort and support for them as well. So instead of yelling at one another because they don't understand how your day went, tell them how bad your day was and what you're worried about for the next day. Better yet, tell them what the *best* part of your day was and allow them to enjoy a piece of that as well. Does that make sense?"

Samantha nodded and she felt Steven reach over for her hand.

"The important thing to remember is to keep coming to the table and keep talking to one another. Communication is key, but so is stating our expectations. Most of the time, disagreements between couples happen from unmet expectations."

Samantha knew that she was guilty of being mad at Steven for not doing what she wanted him to do, even though she never told him. She relied on the concept that "if he loves me, he should just know," but the way that Dr. Bradford explained it, she knew that that wasn't realistic.

Steven squeezed Samantha's hand. "That's something to work on."

CHAPTER 28

- MONDAY -

The bus didn't go *exactly* to Charlie's house, but it got Kathy close enough that she only needed to walk two blocks until she was on his street.

Kathy hadn't been able to stop thinking about Charlie all night. As much as she wanted to move on from him and cut him out of her life for what he'd done the night before, a bigger part of her longed to see him. Longed to be with him.

Maybe that was her problem. She just needed to have sex. Maybe it wasn't Charlie at all.

But the more she thought about it, the more she realized that wasn't true. She had gone months without being with anybody and she had never felt desire quite like this. The way she was feeling was in direct relation to how she felt about

Charlie specifically. And that meant that she needed to see him.

The front door of his house was a large, ornate, solid-wood door. The walkway leading to it was lined with manicured flowers and brick pavers that told any visitor that he had money before they even got in the door. Even though his yard was expansive, the front door was located in a nook created by evergreens that seemed to give a sense of intimacy.

Kathy pressed the button for the doorbell but, unlike her house, she couldn't hear it ring throughout the house from where she stood. She had no idea when to expect anyone to answer the door because she couldn't hear *anything* on the inside. All she heard were birds chirping and the quiet sound of a passing car.

That's why it surprised her when the door suddenly opened and Charlie stood on the other side.

Or maybe part of her surprise was that he answered it with an open robe.

Immediately, her eyes traveled over his body and, much to her delight, he looked much like the dream she had had a few nights ago.

"Kathy, I'm glad you're here." He stepped toward her and reached for her hands.

Her eyes snapped up to his, suddenly remembering that he had some explaining to do. Put pulled her hands away from his reach. "Hold on. It's not going to be that easy."

"I know. I just want you to know that I'm sorry for

everything last night." He stepped aside. "Please, come in."

She shook her head. "No. Because if I come in, then you're going to have me sit down and I'm going to get comfortable and fall victim to your charms."

He leaned against the doorframe. "Then why did you come?"

"Because I believe everyone deserves a second chance." She couldn't help but think of Jeremy and how many chances she had given him. But even though he had broken her heart—on multiple occasions—they still had some very happy moments. Maybe she could make some of her own happy moments with Charlie and they could put last night's argument behind them.

"Well, I appreciate that. Like I said, I'm sorry. Ru—Ruth is an old lover of mine. I didn't realize she still had a key, but this morning I'm going to call a locksmith and have all the locks changed." He shook his head. "What she did was unacceptable and I'm sorry that it caused you pain."

"Then why wouldn't you tell me her name last night?" Kathy asked. "Why didn't you tell me who she was?" Another question burned in her brain: why was he holding her hand? She kept that question to herself, though. She didn't want him to explain it away so easily. She needed to remain guarded. Their relationship was still new.

Another thing she had to keep reminding herself.

Charlie chewed on his bottom lip as he cast his eyes downward. The act made Kathy melt inside. "Honestly, it's because I was hoping that we could salvage the evening between the two of us. I thought that if you knew who Ruth was, that you might be too preoccupied with her to do anything with me."

"Oh." Kathy looked down at his open robe and inspected his body again. It took all of her energy to stand her ground and not jump him right there in the front doorway.

"I called her last night and made it very clear with her that we're done," Charlie said. "There's only room for one woman in my life, Kathy, and that's you." He reached out and tipped her chin up so that she was looking right at him. He leaned in for a kiss, but she backed up.

"Just…one more question. Is Ruth…is she…do you and her have kids together?"

Charlie dropped his head and let out a sigh. "Yes. We do."

"Oh. Okay."

"But I promise you, Kathy, we're only co-parents now. We don't have any romantic connection. Ruth and I are done."

"Is she your ex-wife?"

"Yes."

Somehow, those details made Kathy feel better about all of it. Of course Charlie would need to talk to the mothers of his children. Of course he would still have some sort of contact with his ex-wife. And since his relationship with Kathy was still so new, it was unlikely that Ruth—or any of the other women he had previously been involved with—even knew that Kathy existed. Last night could've just been an honest mistake.

And now Kathy felt embarrassed for the way that she had acted.

Kathy leaned in and kissed him, finally giving in to temptation and sliding her hands against Charlie's nearly-naked body.

Charlie pulled her in for a hug, but then stepped away and tied his robe closed. "I'd like to make this up to you."

"No, you don't have to. It was a misunderstanding. Let's just move on and—"

"Are you free today at all?"

Kathy thought about work. She was already running late. Shirley probably already had to open the office and get the first patients recorded. But it wasn't anything that she couldn't handle on her own. Or *shouldn't* be able to handle on her own.

"No," she told him. "I have nothing to do today."

CHAPTER 29

Since their marriage counseling appointment was first thing in the morning, both Samantha and Steven had only taken the morning off from work. Now they were enjoying lunch together before they went their separate ways for the afternoon.

They sat at a table near the windows at a fast food restaurant down the street from where their appointment had been. Fast food wasn't Samantha's first option, but with the time they had left and the limited options in the area, they really had no other choice.

"I feel like every time we go to see Dr. Bradford, he's yelling at us." Steven pulled the pickles off of his burger.

"He's not *yelling*, Steven. He's trying to help us." Samantha dipped her French fries in her ketchup, then took a bite and felt the sweet tomato taste ignite the corners of her tongue. "All he's doing is pointing out the bad habits that we *both* have that are contributing to our marital problems."

"It just doesn't make me feel good."

"Of course not. He's basically telling us what we're doing wrong. But for me, I'm glad that he's pointing it out because otherwise I wouldn't have realized it."

"Like what?"

She shrugged. "I don't know. I guess just our whole perception of the marriage. We're both in it. We both need to work on it. Yes, of course, things in life are going to come up, but as long as we keep coming back to each other and *trying*, that's all that matters."

He nodded. "I will say, I have been enjoying our dates."

"Even though we haven't been able to *seal the deal* just yet?"

Steven smiled behind his napkin as he wiped the ketchup from his mouth. "Admittedly, that would make them even better, but even without that part figured out yet I'm having a good time."

She couldn't help but return his smile. This was the connection she had missed. The casual rapport they had with one another. The sense of ease that his presence brought her. Her husband, the man she had truly married, had resurfaced. "Me too. It's like, a reminder that I actually like you."

He rolled his eyes with a smile. "And there you had to go

and ruin it. Should we go back and see Dr. Bradford so he can point it out to you?"

She tossed a fry at him. "No, my husband has already *so kindly* called me out on it."

Steven ate the fry that she threw at him. "Well, regardless, we should keep going on these dates. Even if it's a quick lunch date like this. I know Josh makes it a little more complicated, but we have your sister to lean on. And, I promise, the world will not end if my mother watches him too."

She made a face. "Let's not argue. I'm having a good time. But yes, I would like to go on more dates with you."

"On the bright side, even though it's taking us some time to actually *reconnect* the way we want to, all of these dates are really making it worth the wait."

Samantha sat back and watched her husband. It was possibly one of the sweetest things he had said to her and made up for a lot of the issues they had been having. Even as he chowed down on his burger, she couldn't help but sit back and admire him. This was the man that she had devoted her life to. And what a good choice she had made.

CHAPTER 30

Kathy felt the sunshine on her face. For real this time. Just like in her dream, she was wearing a small swimsuit—one that Charlie had bought for her the day before—and drinking a glass of iced tea as she watched the waves on Lake Erie lap up along Charlie's yacht. The boat rocked slightly with the movement. It was peaceful.

Charlie stepped onto the deck wearing a tight, short swimsuit. It was shorter than most of the men her age were wearing nowadays. But then, Charlie was a product of his generation and old habits died hard.

Not that Kathy was complaining about him showing more skin than she was used to. In fact, she was wearing a swimsuit that showed more skin than she usually did when she went to the beach. Maybe he was trying to show off for her like she was trying to show off for him.

He came up behind her and wrapped his arms around her. She leaned back against him, loving the feel of their bare skin pressed together. Of his arms around her. It felt just like her dream. The only difference being that his child wasn't growing in her belly.

"Mmm," she moaned as she nuzzled into his neck.

"Are you enjoying yourself?"

"Very much." She set her glass down on a nearby table, then turned to face him. She wrapped her arms around his neck. "But I could think of something we could be doing that would make this even *more* enjoyable."

Charlie carefully extracted himself from her wandering hands. "As tempting as that is, today is meant to make up for the misunderstanding last night."

She kissed him. "You're forgiven. Now let's go downstairs." She took his hand and tried to lead him toward the stairs, but he pulled her back.

"Kathy, trust me, you're making this very tempting for me." He stood back and took in her figure. "*Very* tempting."

She did a seductive little dance as a way to tempt him further.

"But I want to be sure that we're in good standing before we move this relationship to the next level."

She took his face between her hands. "Charlie, look at me.

We're fine. I'm not mad at you anymore. I get it. And I get it that I'm the only woman in your life. Now take me downstairs and—"

He silenced her with a kiss. "We will. In due time. Right now, let's just enjoy the day on the water together. The sun is shining. The water is calm. We're alone together. There are hardly any other boats out with us. It's perfect."

No other boats? Maybe they didn't even have to go downstairs. They could do it right there on the deck while the sun beat on them and Charlie—

What was wrong with her? Why was she this obsessed with him? But then she looked at him and soon she was wondering what Charlie looked like naked. The way he would be when they were finally alone and she had him just the way she wanted him.

"Kathy, are you listening to me?"

She blinked. "Huh?"

"Where is your head today?"

"Wrapping up in you." She smirked.

Again, he kissed her. "There will be plenty of time for that later, like I said. Besides, when it finally happens, you'll need all of your energy." He planted his lips on hers, and Kathy felt weak in the knees. And everywhere else.

CHAPTER 31

"Is the witch here?" Rusalka stood on the other side of the door at Orias's lake house.

"No, she just left." Orias stood back and allowed her entry. "But even if she was, she would've heard you call her a witch and then this all would've been ruined. Why do you insist on coming back here?"

"It's been two days now since I last visited. I thought that maybe yesterday you would've finished the job."

Orias thought back to yesterday on Lake Erie when he had Kathy in the palm of his hand. He could've had her then, with the way she was throwing herself at him. He thought back to how she was practically prancing around half naked all day. How at any moment, if he would've started to initiate it, she could've been his.

But he wanted to push her a little more. Wine and dine her. Schmooze her. Make her nearly obsessed with him and eager for the first time there were intimate. That *need* to have him would only aid him in his goal of creating offspring.

"No. I'm still working on my plan." He made his way into the bedroom, where his suit for that evening hung on the bathroom door.

"I'm beginning to think that there is no plan," Rusalka said. "That you're just toying with the witch. With us."

He turned on her, raising a finger in her face, which she flinched away from. "No! That is *not* what is happening! I'm trying to secure the future of our harem, of our coven! If I screw this up—or if you screw it up for me—then I will have to spend *even more* time away from you and the girls. Or maybe the witch will just kill me. Is that what you want? Who is going to take care of you and the girls then?"

Rusalka turned into herself. "You're right. I'm sorry, sir. It's just without you to serve, or children to raise, or men to hunt for more children, the girls and I are getting—"

"Bored?"

She shrugged in response. "And that makes us a bit paranoid."

He stepped toward her and grabbed her roughly under the chin and forced his mouth onto hers. "Trust me, when I am able to return home, I am going to make up for the time that we have lost. And, if all goes well, I won't be returning home alone."

"You're going to bring the witch back with you?"

He released her and then returned to his suit. He pulled out the shirt and lay it on the ironing board. "Yes, I will. While she's pregnant, it'll be imperative that we take good care of her until the baby is born. Since she'll be an outsider to our coven, it'll be important for us to make sure the baby stays with us upon its birth."

Rusalka nodded. "I understand. I will return home and prepare the other succubi for another roommate."

"Oh, Kathy won't be a roommate," Orias said as Rusalka turned to leave. "She'll be our prisoner."

CHAPTER 32

- TUESDAY -

The sense of dread filled Samantha as soon as she walked into the dentist office. Even though she wasn't there for a teeth cleaning, that familiar smell reminded her of traumatic experiences she had had when she was a kid and had to have cavities filled. She had never had to have as many filled as Kathy did—which was now ironic given Kathy's place of employment—but she had enough to leave permanent mental scars into her adulthood.

Samantha wanted to take Kathy out for lunch. After Samantha had picked her up from Charlie's house on Sunday, she had told Kathy to call and let her know how things had gone with Charlie and she never did. In fact, the last time Samantha had even spoken to her sister was when she had dropped her off at her apartment Sunday night. Now that it was Tuesday and there was still no word from Kathy, Samantha was growing worried.

The woman sitting behind the desk was picking away at a bag of chips that was cleverly stashed under a pile of folders. As the woman flipped through a magazine in front of her, her hand idly reached out, retrieved another chip, and popped it into her mouth. She showed no sign of acknowledging Samantha's presence.

Samantha cleared her throat. "Excuse me?"

The woman looked up and smiled. The name tag around her neck said her name was Shirley, who Samantha remembered Kathy complaining about when she first started.

"Hi, are you here for an appointment?" Shirley asked.

"No, I was hoping I could talk to my sister, Kathy Walker. Did she already go on lunch?"

Shirley's face dropped. "Oh."

"Is there something wrong?"

"Well…it's just that Kathy hasn't been here *all week*."

Samantha thought it was an odd phrase to use, being that it was only Tuesday, but she pressed on. "What do you mean? She hasn't come to work?"

Behind Shirley, a man in blue scrubs walked up from the back and set a folder in a bin on top of one of the filing cabinets.

"No, it's kind of a touchy subject around here," Shirley said.

"Since she hasn't been here, *I've* needed to pick up *all* of the work!"

Samantha's eyes darted to the hidden bag of chips, but she didn't say anything about it. "Did she call in?"

"Are you talking about Kathy?" the man behind Shirley asked.

Samantha nodded. "Yeah. I'm her sister."

He offered his hand. "I'm Dr. Newberg."

"I had no idea she hasn't been coming to work." Samantha noticed another patient behind her, so she stepped aside to talk to the doctor. However, Shirley still had her attention on their conversation instead of helping the patient.

Dr. Newberg sighed. "It's unfortunate. I love Kathy. She's a great worker, and she's been a huge asset to the office, but—"

"She needs to show up to work," Samantha finished.

"Right. And, I have to hold everyone to the same standards. Unfortunately, there's a policy on no-call-no-shows. She's on thin ice in that regard."

"How many days has she missed?"

"Before this week? Only a few. But after yesterday and today?" He made a face. "One more day like this, and I'll have no choice but to fire her."

CHAPTER 33

- TUESDAY -

The dress made Kathy feel beautiful, sexy, and better than she had felt in a long time. She spun in the mirror a few times, looking at herself from different angles, and considering how to wear her hair so she could make the best impression on Charlie.

Downstairs, she heard someone knocking on her door. She grabbed her shoes from where she had set them on the bed and carried them down with her as she went to answer the door.

It was Samantha.

"Oh. Hi." Kathy turned and set her shoes on the island. "I need to finish getting ready."

"Where are you going?" Samantha set her purse beside

Kathy's shoes and followed her to the bathroom, where she stood in the doorway.

Kathy looked at herself in the mirror, then reached down for her makeup. "Charlie is taking me to this gala tonight. I guess it's super formal."

"I've been trying to call you," Samantha said. "Have you been busy with Charlie?"

Kathy shrugged. She leaned forward as she painted black lines on the edges of her eyes. "Yeah, I've been spending a lot of time with him."

"So much time that you're skipping work?"

Finally, the younger sister looked over at Samantha after hearing the edge to her voice. "Where did you hear that from?"

"I went down to Dr. Newberg's office to talk to you today. I thought the two of us could go get lunch, but apparently you were skipping today."

"First of all, you need to relax." Kathy turned back and reached for another tube from her makeup bag. "And second, so what if I played a little hooky today. What's the big deal?"

"The big deal is that you played hooky *yesterday* too! Kathy, you have bills to pay! You live alone now, which means that I'm not going to be there to pick up the slack for you."

"I'm well-aware of my finances, Sam. Thank you."

"Then why are you being so irresponsible?"

"I'm just having a little fun." Kathy shrugged and glanced at her sister through the mirror. Then she went back to painting her eyes. "Is that so bad? Or do you expect everyone to be as miserable as you?"

Samantha crossed her arms as she let the insult slide. "Go to work. This better be your last *hooky* day, or you'll be fired. That's what Dr. Newberg told me today."

Again, Kathy shrugged.

"That's it? That's your reaction?"

"Sam, it's not like being a receptionist at a dentist office is my *dream job*." She looked in the mirror and mashed her lips together. "Besides, it's not really that big of a deal whether I have a job or not. Charlie has money. He'll take care of me."

Samantha's eyebrows shot up. "You can't base your whole future on a relationship with a guy who you haven't even known for a full week!"

Kathy zipped up her makeup bag and slid on a gold bracelet that sat on the edge of the vanity. "Can we finish this conversation later? Charlie is going to be here anytime now and I don't want to make him wait."

"No, we can't. I don't think you're understanding the severity of this, Kathy. I want to make sure you're actually hearing me and that you're going to think about what I've said."

"I get it. You want me to have a job. Fine. Whatever." She pushed past her sister and went upstairs. From the loft, she looked through the windows. "Oh, Charlie is outside. I have to go."

Samantha went to the door and stood in front of it. As

Kathy came down the stairs, she clasped a necklace around her neck.

"Are you seriously barricading the door? How dramatic."

"You're being irrational."

Kathy slipped her shoes on her feet and balanced as she lifted each foot to tighten the strap. "And blocking my exit is perfectly normal behavior?"

"Make sure you go to work tomorrow and apologize to Dr. Newberg for skipping."

Kathy grabbed her small bag. "For the record, some of those days that I missed were for witch-related things. Should I tell him about that?"

"Of course not."

"Then I don't really see how an apology will serve any purpose."

"Because it sounds nice and it'll help you keep your job."

"Again, my job is more of a necessity than anything. Now, can you please move? I'm going to be late."

"Not until you promise me you'll go to work tomorrow—and every day after that until all of this is behind you."

"Honestly, I was thinking of quitting anyway."

Samantha leaned forward slightly. "You *what*?"

Kathy shrugged. "Yeah. I mean, now that I'm with Charlie, I have options."

"You can't be serious."

Kathy waved her hands, gesturing for Samantha to get out

of the way. "We can talk later. Right now I have to go!"

Samantha's body went slack and she allowed herself to be pushed aside.

Kathy gave her sister a quick hug. "Sorry for bickering. I promise we'll talk about this later. Bye!" She stepped around Samantha and out the door.

CHAPTER 34

- TUESDAY -

The murmur of chatter hit Kathy's ears like a wall of sound when she and Charlie stepped through the doors of the Erie Club downtown. The gala offered a sensory overload with so much to look at. She tried to take in all the wealthy people mingling, the women's dresses, and the beautiful architecture of the lobby with chandeliers, intricate woodwork, and old paintings lining the walls. It was almost too much, but she fought to maintain her cool.

Near the door stood a waiter with a tray of champagne flutes, which he offered to Kathy and Charlie when they entered.

"Thank you," Kathy said as she and Charlie each took one.

Kathy hooked her arm around Charlie's and followed him

as he led her to a group of people standing at the back of the lobby.

"Charlie!" one man said in surprise. "It's been a long time since we've seen you! Where have you been hiding out?" He slapped Charlie on the back and grinned widely.

"Oh, you know, I've been traveling a lot. Keeping my head down and out of trouble."

"And who is this beautiful woman?" Another man from the group asked.

Charlie put his arm around Kathy's back proudly. "This is Kathy Walker. She's my date. Kathy, this here is John Wallace—"

"The mayor," she blurted as she reached out her hand to shake his. She hadn't expected to be a tiny bit starstruck from seeing the mayor. Not that she was an ardent fan of any politician, but it was still disorienting to meet someone she'd only seen in the newspaper or on the news.

"Just started," he said. "Hopefully I don't screw it up."

"And the rest of these guys are not as big of a deal," Charlie joked. He pointed at each person in the group as he named them off. "Tom Keller, the CEO of Hamot Hospital, Orson Brick, a major real estate developer, and Sandy Whitman, the owner of Calitex Technologies, which builds different medical equipment for the western Pennsylvania region."

Kathy shook hands with each of them and smiled. "It's nice to meet all of you."

"So, Charlie, have you been anywhere interesting on your

yacht lately?" Tom Keller asked. "I saw it was back in the marina."

"Not recently," Charlie said. "But I've been taking Kathy out onto the lake. We've been trying to find pockets of time with just the two of us."

"She's a beautiful woman," he said, as if Kathy wasn't standing right there. "Hey, if you have a free weekend, maybe me, you, and John could hit the golf course. Yeah, we'll call Russell Grossman from the county and have him come out too."

"Russell couldn't make it to this?" Charlie asked.

"No, he called me earlier this week and said he'd just have to write a check." John leaned in closer to Charlie. "I think his wife is having an affair and he wanted to sit down with her and explain how to do it more discreetly, if she insists on doing it at all. He wants to run for another term."

Kathy stood by and listened, noting that none of them seemed particularly interested in her. They never asked where she worked, how she and Charlie had met, or anything else about her.

Then again, after John Wallace's comments about Russell Grossman's wife, Kathy wasn't surprised that she was being ignored. Clearly, their respect for women was in the toilet. The fact that they didn't turn their backs on her so they could have a conversation was probably all that she could ask for. Luckily, Charlie wasn't like that.

Still, she was in a beautiful place, sipping the best

champagne she'd ever had, and on the arm of a man she was crazy about. She had had worse evenings in the past.

"I'll have to let you know about that golf trip," Charlie said. "Listen, I want to check out the rest of the party before dinner. If you'll excuse us."

The men all waved to Charlie, then turned away as Kathy put a hand up in a goodbye gesture.

"Sorry about that," he murmured to her when they were out of earshot. "Men in power can sometimes be pigs. Not all of the bigwigs are like that, but that Tom Keller can be. And then he gets the rest of them going."

"That's okay," Kathy said. "This is your world. I expected to just be your date tonight."

"You might not be used to being in my world, but that doesn't mean that you're invisible." He kissed the top of her head.

Kathy felt like she was flying.

They stopped in a wide doorway leading into the large dining room. He kissed her cheek. "Thank you for coming with me."

"Of course."

"These charity events are usually pretty boring," he admitted. "But I thought you'd like this one because, after dinner, they have a DJ and there's dancing."

Kathy smiled. "I like dancing."

"It's not exactly like a club, this is more formal—for the

photos—but I thought it'd be nice to hold you in my arms as we move to the music."

Her heart fluttered. She stretched up on her toes kissed him.

"Uh oh! Caught a little PDA moment," someone said from the dining room. "Don't let Frank from the *Times* see. He'll want a picture for the paper, and then you'll never hear the end of it."

Kathy liked the idea of a photo of her and Charlie kissing at a fancy gala being plastered in the newspaper. It was the same sense of pride that she felt when they had gone out to the mall a few days ago. But Charlie didn't seem like he liked the idea of his romantic relationship being broadcasted. In fact, he seemed very private about a lot of things. It was a nice change of pace for Kathy.

"I don't think letting *Robert Calloway* see that little kiss was a very smart move, either," Charlie said.

Kathy took a closer look and saw that, indeed, it was Robert Calloway, from the six o'clock news. "Oh wow!"

He shook Kathy's hand, but looked to Charlie for the introduction, which he provided.

"Nice to meet you," Robert said to Kathy. "I wish I was on duty today so I could capture this beautiful face."

"Are you here representing the station?" Charlie asked.

Robert nodded. "Yeah. The general manager couldn't make it, so he wanted to send me. Said he thought my face would be more memorable than his absence."

"There's an ego boost that you especially don't need."

The newscaster laughed and jabbed Charlie playfully in the stomach. "Ah, you got jokes! I was happy to come, though. It got me out of the evening news for one night."

"Yeah, I was surprised that a gala like this is on a Tuesday night," Kathy said.

"They've moved the date all around over the last few years," Robert said. "They thought a Saturday would be nice, but then some major stakeholders couldn't make it. Then they did a Friday and others couldn't make it. Then a Monday, and almost nobody showed up. I guess they were thinking that on a Tuesday people are willing to come and spend their money without the workweek tying them up, and without weekend getaways preventing people from attending."

"Events like this are all about the money," Charlie said. "It's a charity for the hospital, so if they schmooze the rich people enough, they're more likely to write even fatter checks."

"I guess that's true," Kathy said. "And from the sound of it, these types of people tend to travel more, which makes sense that weekends aren't ideal for this event."

Robert nodded. "Weekenders. Some of them fly to New York every weekend. If you ask me, I think a lot of them have second families out there that don't know anything about their families here."

Kathy's eyes widened. "Really?"

He shrugged. "Just a theory. Hasn't been proven. And you did *not* hear it from me."

"Anyway," Charlie said as a change of subject. "They added dancing a few years ago as a way to draw out the wives."

"Men are more likely to come if their wives are dragging them," Robert added. "And women are more generous than men. Throw up some sad looking pictures of sick kids and the women are all begging their husbands to pull out their wallets."

"That seems…sexist," Kathy said.

Charlie nodded. "Sure it is, but it's also effective." He finished his champagne and handed it to the nearest waiter wandering the room. "Kathy, let's find our seats. Robert, it was nice talking to you."

"See you, Charlie." Robert walked off with a wave.

Kathy allowed Charlie to lead her into the dining room, where there were many more people mingling and chatting around the round tables with white tablecloths and candles in the center. Each place setting had names printed on little tags, indicating where each person was supposed to sit.

As she held Charlie's hand and followed him through the world completely different than her own, she couldn't help but feel like this was a life she could get used to. The wife of a wealthy man. Charlie Parrish's wife.

That was a title she would certainly be very proud to have.

CHAPTER 35

- TUESDAY -

The pages of *The Art of Magic* crinkled as Samantha sifted through them. She skimmed each one before flipping to the next.

Steven came into the living room and plopped on the opposite end of the couch. "Well, the dishes are done. And Josh is asleep."

"Mm-hmm," Samantha murmured, keeping her eyes on the book. "Thanks." She barely registered what he had said. She was so focused on finding something that would explain Kathy's behavior. Sure, she was impulsive, and certainly a romantic, but her complete and sudden devotion to someone she just happened to bump into at the library was alarming. There *had* to be something magical behind it.

"At the risk of starting an argument," Steven started, "let me just ask one question: are our evening plans about to be ruined?"

There was a pause before Samantha registered that she had been asked a question. Finally, she looked up at him. "Hmm?"

He indicated the book. "No offense or anything, but I hate that book. Whenever you pull it out, it means something bad is happening."

She sighed and sat back on the couch, her arms resting on the large book. "Sorry."

"*Is* something bad happening?"

"I don't know. I'm not sure yet."

"What's wrong?"

"There's something going on with Kathy," she said. "Or…I *think* there is."

"Something…magical?"

Samantha shook her head. "I'm not sure. I just know that Kathy's been acting strange lately. She's *obsessed* with this Charlie guy that she's dating."

"Well, I wouldn't worry about it too much. Kathy's always hunting for someone to date. She's sure had her fair-share of boyfriends, even in the time that *I've* known her."

Another shake of her head. "This is different. I agree, Kathy can be boy-crazy, sure, but at the heart of it all, what Kathy's really after is love. She doesn't date just to sleep with them and move on. She wants to settle down with someone. She wants someone permanent. Something like what we have."

Steven grinned. Their marriage may be going through a rough patch, but it was still pretty solid. Enviable by others. That had to count for something.

"But you don't think that's her motivation behind that with this new guy?" he asked.

"No, I don't."

Steven made a face. "But isn't that completely out of your ability to know? Even with your telepathic abilities?"

She looked at her husband. "For the record, I didn't read her thoughts. I *do* have self-control, thank you. No, this feeling I have, it comes from being her sister, not from being telepathic." She turned back to the book and continued flipping.

"Okay, so what about this seems different to you?"

She shrugged. "I don't know! I guess it just seems like this is more fueled by lust than love. And it's having repercussions into her life."

"Well, sometimes lust leads into love," Steven said. "An intense immediate attraction can turn into a lifelong committed relationship."

"This is different. I just know it."

Steven leaned back and put his feet up on the coffee table. "I wouldn't look too much into it. Maybe Kathy just really likes this guy. And maybe *you* don't, which is giving you bad vibes."

"I've never met the guy."

"Doesn't mean you don't have an opinion about him."

"True, but my opinion isn't based on this Charlie guy," Samantha said. "It's how Kathy's acting around him. She's going to get fired from her job because of this obsessive fascination with him—a *stranger* who she's only known for about a week. I admit, she moves quick with men, but she's gone from zero to one hundred *really* fast. Too fast. Even for Kathy."

"Okay, but think of it from her perspective. Like you said, she sees us, married, with a baby and maybe she wants the same—"

"Wait a minute." Samantha stopped on a page that suddenly brought everything into focus.

"What is it?" Steven sat up and tried to look over at the book. "Did you find something?"

Samantha didn't immediately answer. Her eyes scanned the page, then reread it more carefully. When she finally looked up at her husband, who was sitting in anxious anticipation, she said, "That's it. Charlie must be an incubus."

CHAPTER 36

Kathy laughed as Charlie dipped her on the dance floor. She hadn't danced quite like this since the formal high school dances, but she realized now that she missed the intimacy of holding someone close and moving in reaction to them.

It was like she and Charlie were the perfect pair. And she never wanted him as badly as she did right now.

Leaning in close to his ear, she murmured, "I'm having a great time with you. Thanks for bringing me."

"Of course. I wouldn't *dream* of bringing anyone else."

Kathy felt heat flush inside her again. She looked around at the thinning crowd. There were a few other dancers, but the dance floor had dwindled significantly over the last two songs. Her own feet were getting sore. "I don't mean to rush things, but it looks like the party is winding down. What do you say we head back to your place?"

He pulled back enough to raise his eyebrows at her. "Are you sure?"

"Absolutely."

With a smile, he pulled her by the hand and led her toward the exit.

"Leaving already?"

They both stopped in their tracks and saw Tom Keller with a drink in his hand and a cigar pinched between two fingers. He stood at the bar with his elbow propped up. By the look in his eyes, he had had a few drinks since the start of the evening.

"Yeah, it's getting late," Charlie said.

Tom barked out a laugh. "It's only ten o'clock! This party might be winding down, but you know there's always an after-party on my boat."

Charlie looked back at Kathy for an excuse not to go, but she came up short.

"Tom! There you are."

Another man walked up. Kathy remembered him from that first group of men she had met when they first arrived at the party. Orson Brick.

"I've been looking all over for you. Your secretary left with the night's donations already, but we have a few more people who have written checks. Did she go back to her office or did she go home?"

Tom grumbled and took a puff of his cigar before setting his glass down on the bar. "Damn her. I think she was going to go home, but let me call the office to be sure she's not processing any of it until we have the *total* donation amount." He turned and stalked out of the room with Orson in tow.

"Now's our chance," Charlie said with a smirk. "Let's make a break for it." Again, he led Kathy by the hand out into the main foyer, where they were again prevented from exiting at the door.

"Did you two get your party favors?" a woman called to them.

Charlie put up a hand to silently acknowledge that he had heard her but that they weren't interested.

"Ah, there you are!" John Wallace stood outside the front door on the stone porch. "I hope the two of you had a good time."

Kathy nodded. "It was a lot of fun."

"Are you waiting for everyone else to clear out before you go home?" Charlie asked.

John nodded. "It looks bad if I leave before most of the guests. I've tried sneaking out the back before, but I always got a phone call from Tom the next morning calling me out on it. So now I'm just hanging out here. Are you going to the after-party?"

Charlie shook his head. "I don't think we're going to make it."

Mayor Wallace's eyes flittered to Kathy, then back to Charlie. "Ah, I see."

Kathy felt a little exposed that her and Charlie's evening plans were so blatantly obvious, but at the moment what was most pressing to her was getting Charlie alone. And, based on how some of the men had treated her throughout the evening, she knew they already had a low opinion of her simply because she was a woman.

"Anyway, I'll catch up with you later," Charlie said. "Give me a call and maybe we'll hit the golf course sometime."

"Will do." He shook Charlie's hand and patted him on the arm as he walked back.

Charlie and Kathy practically ran down the front steps to the sidewalk. As they turned left onto Peach Street, they only made it a little bit before someone else stood in their way: Samantha.

CHAPTER 37

"Sam? What are you doing here?" Kathy asked.

"He's not who you think he is, Kathy." The elder witch studied her sister and hated seeing her hand locked in his, now that she knew who he was. Or rather, *what* he was. What was worse was that Samantha noticed the incubus squeeze Kathy's hand tighter.

From the Erie Club, people poured out and cars lined up and down Peach Street, waiting to pick up guests from the gala.

Samantha indicated the alley between the Erie Club and the neighboring building. "Back here. We can talk more privately." She started to head in that direction, but the incubus stayed where he was.

"No. I'm not going anywhere with you."

Kathy tugged on his arm. "Charlie, it's okay."

"It's not! This woman is crazy!"

"She's my sister." They stared at each other for a long time before Kathy successfully got him to move into the alleyway.

Samantha followed behind them. "Stay where I can see you. And take your hands off of her!"

"Sam, what's going on? This is Charlie. The guy I've been seeing."

"I know who he is, Kathy. I'm doing this for your own good. I promise."

"You're freaking me out!"

"Just let go of his hand."

"No!"

With no other choice, Samantha squirted the bottle of holy water on the incubus. She had picked it up from a local church on the way downtown, just as the magic book had instructed. His skin sizzled and he cried out in pain.

Kathy turned and let go of his hand so she could reach for his shoulders and hold him steady as he crumpled over in pain. "Charlie! What's wrong?" She turned on Samantha. "What did you *do* to him?"

"He's a demon. And I just revealed that." She pointed in his direction. "See for yourself."

The younger witch slowly turned back and saw the bony, skeletal entity who stood before her. Thin, ragged hair fell around his face, his small body seemed weak and feeble with every joint, bone, and sinew showing with horrid detail. His skin was a very pale white everywhere, except his stomach, which was a warm shade of pink, nearly red.

"This is his true form, Kathy," Samantha said. "He's an incubus. He doesn't love you. He's not capable of it. He's a monster who wants to have sex with you so you can bear his child."

Kathy froze where she was as she eyed the incubus. He started to reach for her, but Samantha shot more holy water at him.

"Get away from her!" she shouted.

"No!" Kathy stepped in front of him with her arms out. "No, *you* get away from him!"

Samantha's eyes turned to concern. Worry. Her baby sister was *protecting* this monster. "Kathy, don't let his sweet-talking fool you. The seduction, the endless thoughts of him, your sudden *obsession* with him? Those are all at the hands of his powers! He's been trying to seduce you. To get you to have sex with him. That's where you were in a rush to get to tonight, wasn't it? And after he was done with you, he would've killed you. Because that's what he does. Take a look at his belly. It's permanently stained from the blood of his victims. And you were about to be one of them."

Kathy stared at the cracked pavement of the alley and slowly shook her head. "No. No! If this is who Charlie is—" She turned and looked back at him. At his true skeletal, demonic form. "Then I accept him. Because I love him."

CHAPTER 38

- TUESDAY -

"**Y**ou *love* him?" Samantha didn't even try to keep the disgust from her voice—or her face. "Kathy, don't be ridiculous! *Look* at him! He's a monster!"

"And the same could be said for us, Sam! Think of what people would say if they saw us using magic and they didn't understand what we stood for? Do you think they'd accept us? Do you think they'd still *like* us?"

Samantha had to admit that her sister had a point. But she didn't dare say that out loud. "That's different, Kathy."

"You're right. This is my life and this is who I choose." Kathy reached back and took the incubus's bony hand.

"Are you, though?"

"Am I *what*?"

"Are you choosing him on your own?"

"What are you talking about? Of course I am!"

"Do you even know what an incubus does?"

The incubus put up his bony free hand to ward off Samantha. "That's enough!" Turning back to Kathy, he shapeshifted back into the attractive older gentleman that had first walked out of the Erie Club with her.

The charm.

The elegance.

The charisma.

"Look at me," he instructed of her.

"Kathy, don't!" Samantha pleaded. "Look at me instead. And listen." When she had her sister's attention, she said, "An incubus's mission is to find women, use their supernatural powers of lust and seduction to get them to have sex with them. He wants you to have a baby with him, Kathy! A *demon* baby!"

The incubus gently cradled the younger witch's chin, turning her head to face him. "Isn't that what you want too, Kathy?" His voice was gentle. Sweet. His words laced with lust. "A baby with me? We haven't really talked about it, but I know you've been thinking about it. You can be my wife. We can be a family."

"Kathy, don't listen to him! This is his power talking! He's trying to manipulate you!"

"Who is the one more likely to lie to you?" he asked Kathy, not even turning to look at Samantha. "The man who has done nothing but love you, or the jealous sister who hates to see you happy?"

Kathy looked at Samantha. "You haven't liked Charlie from the beginning."

"That's not true. I was just nervous because it's been so fast. How long have you even known him?"

"Long enough for me to make my decision." Kathy held up her intertwined hand with the incubus's. "And I choose him."

"Kathy—"

In a flash, the incubus was standing in front of Samantha. Then, just as quickly, the world around her whooshed by as he pushed her out to the edge of the alley with a force that tossed her back onto the sidewalk.

As Samantha rushed to get to her feet, she looked back and saw the incubus standing side-by-side with Kathy again, their hands once again clasped against each other's.

Kathy looked up at him with a glazed look that told Samantha that her sister wasn't in full control of her body. Of her actions. Meanwhile, the incubus smiled down at Kathy with a look of victory. Of triumph.

Finally, Kathy turned back to her sister. "Don't follow me. I've made my choice."

In the next moment, incubus and witch both faded out in a puff of smoke.

CHAPTER 39

- TUESDAY -

Kathy loved feeling Charlie's weight on top of her as they kissed back at his house. Her hands trailed up along his arms, across his back, and down to where his legs straddled her body. Clothes were quickly peeling off one-by-one. The two of them were finally giving in to their desires. It was something that Kathy had wanted for a long time—well, as long as she had known him, which admittedly wasn't long. Samantha had a point about that.

But even though Kathy had only known Charlie for about a week, she knew all she needed to know about him. He was thoughtful, educated, kind, a good listener. She enjoyed spending time with him. And he took care of her.

Why would she walk away from that?

And why would Samantha take issue with Kathy finding comfort in a man like that?

Kathy moaned as Charlie's kisses moved down to her neck. She wrapped her naked leg around his waist and pulled him closer as her hands snaked through his hair.

His body was everything she had envisioned it to be. Of course, she had seen glimpses of it on the boat several times, but there was something about having him—and his body—right there at her disposal made it all the more appealing.

A sudden flash in her mind revealed the form he had taken in the alley. The skeletal, lanky, pale version that looked like—

"Are you okay?" Charlie stopped long enough to look at her.

She smiled. Her body had barely tensed up at the intrusive thought and yet he picked up on it. He knew her better than she knew herself. Samantha's concerns were nothing to be worried about. Charlie loved Kathy. And she knew she could trust him.

Kathy pushed Charlie over onto his back and straddled him.

"Oh, I like where this is going," he said with a smile.

She bit her bottom lip, reveling in his natural good looks. But as she leaned down to kiss those sweet, plump lips of his, she swore she saw him shift back into that scrawny, terrifying *thing*.

It was only for a second, but she was sure she saw it. Either way, it made her pause.

"What's wrong?"

"I don't know." Kathy pinched the bridge of her nose and

squeezed her eyes shut. "I just…thought I saw something."

Charlie's hands wrapped around her waist. "Well, let me take your mind off of it."

He pulled her closer. Just before their lips touched, she saw it again. Longer, this time. Long enough for her to truly believe that she was seeing what she was seeing.

And that she was about to *kiss* the ghostly-white horror that lay before her.

"Ah!" She jumped off the bed, nearly tripping over the sheets that had tangled around her foot in the heat of their passion. Passion that was very rapidly slipping away.

"What's the matter?" He sat up, looking like the Charlie she knew again. His skin shone with sweat that glistened across his muscled chest. The way he propped himself up on his elbows made his abs looked more taut, which only drew attention to other things further south on his body.

And yet, with all of that, Kathy couldn't get the image of the skeletal creature out of her head.

She began to pick her clothes up from the floor and pull them back on. "I don't…I don't think I can do this. Not today. I'm sorry."

He stood and hurried to her. "Kathy, come on. Don't be ridiculous. This is what we both want."

She pressed her hands against his chest. It was firm. Strong. Tanned. Nothing like that other way she had seen him, but she couldn't get it out of her mind.

"Don't let what your sister said scare you. Make your own choice."

"I know. She doesn't understand us."

"Then what's the matter?" He leaned in and kissed her neck again. She felt herself go weak, but her eyes flickered open for a second and she saw pale white skin again, a knotted spine, and every rib protruding through his sickly skin from his back.

She screamed again and backed away, hurrying to get back into her dress.

"Kathy, I don't understand what's going on." He grabbed her arm, squeezing tighter than she felt comfortable with. It was possessive, almost aggressive. Controlling. She didn't like that one bit.

She looked into his eyes—the eyes she had gotten to know over the last week—and yet, she didn't like what she saw in them anymore. The Charlie she knew wouldn't grab her like this. He wouldn't push her to do anything she wasn't comfortable with. Especially sex.

"Let me go," she said.

"No. Not until you tell me what's going on."

"I want to go home."

"No, you don't. You want me!"

Her heart raced and suddenly all traces of the arousal she had been feeling moments before were replaced with fear.

"You're not going anywhere until you have sex with me."

Kathy stared at him. Not only was she surprised that those

words had left his mouth, but she was terrified as to what he was going to make her do. "Let me go, before I call the police!"

"The police can't save you, honey." His voice sounded contorted. As if strained. Unnatural. Nothing like the sweet, warm baritone that he usually had. He moved in to kiss her again.

She tried to back away, but she backed into the wall. He had her pinned. She put up her free hand and froze him where he was.

With him immobilized, she let out a breath of relief, but felt her hand still in his frozen grasp. How was she going to get out of this?

She didn't have to think of an answer for long, though. Seconds after freezing Charlie, she felt herself magically disappearing from the room altogether.

CHAPTER 40

- TUESDAY -

Samantha breathed a sigh of relief when she saw her sister materialize in front of her. After Kathy and the incubus had disappeared, she feared the worst. Then she had remembered something she had read in *The Art of Magic* and raced over to Perry Square, just across the street from the Erie Club. "It worked!"

Kathy looked around as she fished for the zipper on the back of her dress. Now that she was suddenly in a public place, she wanted to put herself back together as quickly as possible, especially considering the state she had been in only moments before.

"Are you okay?"

Kathy nodded. "I'll be fine. He's pissed, though."

"I figured he would be. Are you okay now? You're not still wanting to go back to him are you?"

She shook her head. "No. I see him for what he is now. What did you do? How did I get here? One minute I was so into—" she stopped and amended, "under his spell, then the next minute I saw his true form and was kind of revolted by him. That's when he started getting angry."

"Because his hold on you was slipping." Samantha went behind her sister to help her with the zipper. She noted that Kathy didn't have any shoes on. "I used my telepathy to help bring out clarity in your mind. It was there, but the incubus had buried it so far deep in your mind that it took some work to get it out to the surface of your consciousness."

"And you did all of that from here?"

Samantha nodded.

"You've never been able to extend your power that far before."

"I know. I think it's because I tapped into my connection with you as my sister." She took Kathy's hands. "Now, come on, we need to hurry because he'll be here soon."

No sooner had the words left her mouth that the incubus appeared—in all his true form glory—in a puff of smoke.

Samantha took a brief survey of the few people in the park. There were some people by the fountain, others sleeping on park benches. Her eyes glanced over to the Erie Club, where most of the gala attendees had cleared out.

It wasn't ideal, being out in a public setting, but at least nobody was looking directly at them. For the time being, at least.

"It's over," Samantha said.

The incubus laughed. "You can't stop me!" He waved his bony arms out. "Look around! There are plenty of other women I can find! Someone who doesn't have any idea of who I am or what I want from her."

"That's never going to happen." Samantha handed a piece of paper to Kathy. "Start the spell."

"No! You won't touch him!" a woman's voice from behind the sisters drew their attention.

Samantha turned and saw a beautiful woman walking up to them.

"Ruth," Kathy breathed. "Is she...? You're just like him, aren't you?"

"A succubus?" the woman said, as she came around the sisters. "Yes. And I'm not going to let you kill my man."

"Rusulka, stand down," the incubus told her. "I'm in control here."

"Start the spell," Samantha said to her sister again.

Kathy watched for a moment before her eyes traveled to Rusulka, then she raised the spell and began to recite it.

Liar, fraud, cheater, flirt.
Playing with the heart's desire.

"You're wasting your time!" the incubus called out. "I can only be killed on consecrated ground."

"I know," Samantha said, then turned to finish the spell.

No longer will you hurt.
Death takes you with this fire.

The incubus was flung backward and pressed flat against the pedestal of the Civil War Memorial. Flames surrounded him as his body burned. The light from the fire shone throughout the park, illuminating the dark night, but the sisters were standing far enough away that the onlookers didn't notice them. Only the flame.

"No!" Rusulka cried out. She turned on the sisters. "What did you do?"

Samantha looked around nervously. They were gaining the attention of the quiet park. "Um…what do we do?"

Kathy looked down at the spell and recited it again.

Liar, fraud, cheater, flirt.
Playing with the heart's desire.
No longer will you hurt.
Death takes you with this fire.

Rusulka was suddenly pulled back in her pursuit of the

sisters and slammed against the pedestal of the same monument where the incubus had burned only moments before.

As the flames consumed her, she let out a shriek that echoed throughout the park.

Samantha grabbed Kathy's hand and slowly pulled her back toward the forming crowd, who were all staring at the scorch marks left on the monument.

The sisters faded into the crowd, then slowly made their way to the sidewalk and down to where Samantha had parked.

CHAPTER 41

"Let me walk you up." Samantha turned off the car outside of Kathy's apartment and got out onto the street. It was a warm night, and actually very pleasant, if it wasn't for the incubus vanquish.

"Sam, you don't have to do that," Kathy said, even as she led her sister into the building.

"I think we need to talk," Samantha said. "We're long-overdue."

The two of them made their way up to Kathy's apartment. Samantha took a seat on the couch while Kathy poured each of them water.

"Is water okay or is this a wine conversation?"

Samantha smiled. "No, water's fine. I can't stay too long

anyway. Steven will be worried. Besides that, I need to get some sleep for work tomorrow."

Kathy took a seat on the other end of the couch. "I'm sorry for ruining your Tuesday."

"Don't be. I'm sorry I didn't see that you were in trouble sooner."

The younger sister took a sip of her water. "Once again, I fell prey to another man."

"That's a little harsh on yourself, don't you think?"

"Maybe, but it's true." Kathy shot her sister a look, signaling that nothing needed to be said for Samantha to agree. "If Charlie taught me anything, it's that it's okay to give in to your heart's desire sometimes. I mean, obviously he had me under a spell and he was just trying to get me in bed, but I still felt that rush of a new relationship. Of wanting to spend all of my time with someone. Exploring new things, meeting new people. And the *clothes*! I don't know where he got the money, but at least I upgraded my wardrobe after this whole mess."

Samantha smiled. "I guess that's a positive. Kathy, it sounds like what you're really looking for is someone to spend your life with. I know you've been in kind of a funk since you and Jeremy split up, but what *I'm* seeing from this whole ordeal is that you *wanted* to be in a relationship. You wanted Charlie to be as genuine as you saw him."

"Well, in my defense, he put on a very good act. But you're right, it was nice being on someone's arm again. I do miss that."

"You'll find someone. You just need to give it some time." Samantha watched her sister for a moment, debating whether she should say the next thing, then deciding it was better said than unsaid. "One thing you can do now to get your life back in order is to go to bed so you can get to work on time tomorrow."

Kathy cringed. "Yeah. About that…"

Samantha looked nervously at her sister. "What?"

"I think I'm going to quit."

"Kathy!"

"I hate it, Sam! I mean, I guess I don't *hate* it, but it's so boring. I just feel like I'm wasting my time there."

Samantha sat back and sighed. She pinched the bridge of her nose while she bit back her tongue to keep her comments to herself.

"I need to stop being someone that I'm not," Kathy went on. "That's how I got into this mess with Charlie in the first place. I was looking for some excitement in my life and Charlie was the first person to offer that to me."

"So what are you going to do for work, then?"

Kathy shrugged. "I don't know."

"Then how are you going to keep paying the rent on this place?"

"Well, that's the other thing…" She let out a deep breath. "I was thinking that while I start figuring out who I am and what I'm going to do with my life, I can move back in with you and Steven."

"Kathy, you're the one who wanted to move out."

"I know! But one of the things I've learned from living alone is that I still need the guidance of my sister."

"We can still have a relationship even though we're living apart. Literally everyone does it, Kathy. It's called growing up."

"But not everyone is a witch."

Samantha rocked her head back and forth.

"Admit it, you would like it if I moved back in. I could help run the errands, keep the house clean, watch Josh. I mean, you and Steven would save a fortune on daycare if I was watching him all day."

"So you're going to quit your job and give up your independence to babysit?"

"To reconnect with my family. I don't see you as much as I would like. Every time I see Josh, I swear he's a different baby."

Samantha still wasn't convinced. "It's not that I'm against you moving back in, it's just that I'd hate to see you give up good things in your life to go backwards."

"But it'd be going *forward*," Kathy said. "I wouldn't be tied down by responsibilities. I would have the freedom to figure out what exactly I want to do with my life. I *wish* I was like you and knew what I wanted and then just go out and get it, but let's face it, Sam. I'm not you. I'm not that driven. I've had countless jobs, went to college for a bit, and even got a place of my own. None of it is really clicking for me. I need to figure out why that is."

"I get that. But to be fair, I didn't really have a choice. When

Dad disappeared, I was in college and I *needed* to work and get a good job so that we could keep the house. We *both* had to work. I don't ever want to go back to that, but that means that I need to make certain sacrifices to maintain our lifestyle and our family."

Kathy nodded. "I know. And I know it's unfair that, as the oldest, you needed to give up so much. But look what you have as a result of those sacrifices? You have Steven and Josh and a job you're good at. And you're *still* in that house."

"Our house," Samantha said. "It will always be your home too."

"So I have your support?"

Samantha studied her sister. "Yeah, you do. I may not agree with it, but I understand it."

"Thank you!" Kathy scooted to the end of the couch and hugged her sister's arm. "Wait, do you think Steven will be okay with this? I know he was happy to get rid of me."

"He'll get over it. But…maybe don't tell him that you're *quitting* your job. It might be better if he thinks that the incubus made you *lose* your job. I'll work on winning him over with the rest of it."

CHAPTER 42

- TUESDAY -

It was late by the time Samantha got back home. After brushing her teeth and changing into her pajamas, she crawled into bed slowly to avoid waking Steven.

Once she was under the covers, though, she felt him roll over and wrap his arms around her.

"How did everything go?" he grumbled sleepily near her ear.

"Good. Kathy's safe." For a moment, she considered mentioning to him that Kathy was going to move back in, but she decided that that was a conversation for another time.

"That's good." Steven kissed her cheek. "I'm glad you're safe too."

She turned her head to kiss his lips. No matter their issues, his lips would always feel like home. And, after Kathy's reminder that Samantha had a lot of good things in her life, she decided to lean in to the kiss and it became more intense.

He backed off and looked at her in the darkness. "Is this the perfect time to…reconnect?"

Samantha thought about the time. She thought about work. She thought about how early Josh would get up or how tired she would be the next day. But none of that mattered. She wasn't going to worry about any of that at the moment because all she wanted was her husband. And he wanted her. The rest could wait.

"It's as good a time as any."

Steven kissed her again. "I feel like we're in a better place now, aren't we?"

She couldn't help but laugh. The stars had aligned and they were finally going to do the thing that they had been trying to do for a week, and *now* he wanted to talk?

"What?" he asked, suddenly self-conscious.

"Nothing. I agree. I think we're heading in the right direction."

"We know where we both stand and there's no secrets between us."

Samantha's smile faded and she was grateful for the darkness to hide it. There were some secrets still, but that was an issue for tomorrow. Tonight, they were content. She pulled her husband to her and kissed him.

Incubus

As he moved down to kiss her neck, she thought of the two biggest secrets she was keeping from him.

Kathy moving back in with Samantha giving her permission without even talking to Steven first. That was something she would tell him sooner than later, and she knew it would result in a fight, but Steven wouldn't put up too much of a fuss. He knew how much Kathy meant to her and, when presented with the cost savings for daycare, he would come around.

The other secret, perhaps the biggest, was that Josh was a witch and would someday develop powers of his own, just like his mother. Samantha wasn't sure how she was going to tell Steven about that. Worse, she wasn't sure how he would react to that news. That thought alone scared her. She wondered if she should've been upfront about it when she first got pregnant, but she couldn't imagine a world without Josh in it. A world without their perfect little family in it.

"No secrets," Samantha murmured in his ear.

As Steven's hands explored her body, in her ear he murmured, "I love you so much."

But would he love her when the truth came out?

"I love you too."

ACKNOWLEDGMENTS

This project would not have been possible without the support of my Kickstarter backers! Thank you all for your support!

Sarah B.

Gee Rothvoss

Leslie Twitchell

Marlene Renteria

Samantha Newberry

Dead Fish Books

Rowan Stone

Lou Paduano

John Idlor

Gary Phillips

Shanon M. Brown

Thank you to the DN Publishing VIP Club members over at Patreon!

Tracy O'Neil

Marguerite Goosby

patreon.com/DNPublishing

Beware the enemy who hides in plain sight.

Samantha and Kathy head to Shady Acres, owned by the Fisher family, for a weekend getaway in the mountains. As soon as they get there, both of them have an uneasy feeling about their hosts.

But their cabin is located deep in the woods, far away from the Fisher house, so they decide to make the best of their weekend. And they do have a good time…until the Fishers chase them out of their cabin and into the woods in the middle of the night.

It doesn't take long before the sisters realize they're being hunted like animals for sport. They quickly discover that they're not the first ones this has happened to.

And the worst part? The Fishers are completely human.

Human is the thirteenth book in the Coven series, which is part of the Art of Magic universe, containing the Lost By Magic and the Under the Moon series.

HUMAN

COVEN: BOOK 13

Read on for an excerpt of the next book in
the Coven series!

DAVID NETH

CHAPTER 1

- OCTOBER 1990 -

As the rain hit the metal roof of the cabin, the sound ricocheted, bringing with it a peaceful white noise that seemed to cap the perfect day. The Williamsons had enjoyed a day of hiking, and had even cooked their lunch on a campfire just outside the cabin. It had been a warm fall day, which they were happy to spend as a family over the long weekend. Just one more night and then they'd be home and ready to jump back into their weekly routines.

With night quickly enveloping the sky, Lynn fussed with the propane stove at the small kitchenette inside the cabin. It had been heating just fine a minute ago, but now it seemed like everything was cooling off.

Her eight-year-old daughter, Crystal, lay on the couch near

the dying fire. Lynn watched as she tried to read her book in the dim light. The lightbulbs around the room didn't cast very much light throughout the cabin.

"Honey, can you even see the words on the pages?"

Crystal squinted. "Not really. And it's getting colder."

Lynn turned to her husband, who sat at the table beside the fire reading the newspaper.

"Larry, why don't you go out and get some firewood to restock the fire?" she suggested. "We don't want the temperature to drop too low in here overnight. It's supposed to dip down into freezing tonight. Oh, and see if you can spot a propane tank out on the porch or something. I think this one's out of juice."

"I didn't see an extra one."

She sighed and put one hand on her hip while the other poked at their dinner on the small skillet. "Can you please go check? Unless you'd rather eat half-cooked burgers for dinner."

He sighed heavily as he closed the newspaper with a loud crinkle. "I suppose, dear." He stood and reached his arms upward in a stretch. He held it for a few seconds before proceeding across the room and to the door.

They were all tired from hiking, and they were starting to snap at each other. That's why Lynn wanted to get everyone fed and keep them warm to prevent anymore snipes caused by hunger or discomfort. Herself included. They had had such a perfect weekend that she'd hate to see it ruined on their last night.

The cold air filled the room as Larry opened the door. The outer screen door slapped against the wood frame in his departure. There was a part of Lynn that loved that sound. As a kid, her parents would take her and her brother camping like this all the time. They often went in the summer time, but Lynn particularly loved those fall trips with the morning dew, the smell of the leaves, and the chill in the air.

Now that Lynn had a family of her own, she was insistent that those camping trips continue. And for the most part, Larry and Crystal loved the trips just as much.

The door swung open again and Larry quickly came inside. The screen door slapped against the frame again behind him. Softer this time, since Larry had closed the inner door so quickly and pressed his back against it.

"What's the matter?" Lynn saw the look of concern in her husband's eyes. Adding to that was his empty hands. Why hadn't he grabbed the wood that had been sitting just outside the door on the porch?

Larry locked the door. "Turn out the lights! Get down beneath the windows!"

Crystal sat up in the couch and looked at her father, then to her mother for reassurance. Panic was stricken across her face.

Lynn was annoyed at her husband for scaring their daughter, although by the look in her husband's face, she was starting to believe that he was serious. "Larry, what's—"

"Get down!"

Wordlessly, Lynn crossed the room to her daughter and led her to the front windows, where they lowered themselves down beneath the sill.

Larry peered through the window at the top of the door, then slunk down beside his family. "You didn't turn off the light!"

"You never told me what's going on," she countered.

Crystal brought her knees to her chest. "Mommy, what's going on?"

Lynn wrapped her arm tighter around her daughter. "I don't know, baby. It'll okay, though. It'll all be—"

"Shh!" Larry put a finger behind his ear, then whispered, "You hear that?"

Lynn's stomach dropped. She certainly did hear it. Voices. Men's voices. Just outside their windows.

Crystal huddled closer to her mother, quietly whimpering.

"It's okay. We'll all be okay." Lynn knew that nobody was buying her words—not even herself—but, as a mother, she felt them instinctively flow out of her.

The voices faded. The three of them sat in the growing darkness in silence. Even the single lightbulb hanging from the ceiling was flickering, as if it was about to go out.

Lynn made eye contact with her husband and mouthed: *Are they gone?*

Larry turned and peered out the window. Just a smidgen

at first, then he sat up straighter, allowing himself in full view of the window.

"You're scaring your daughter," Lynn said. The annoyance came from her hunger. Although her own fear was probably a factor too.

Larry fell back onto the floor and rested against the wall. He patted Crystal's leg. "I'm sorry, sweetie. It's okay. I just thought—well, it doesn't matter anymore. I was just overreacting."

"So there's no one outside?" Crystal asked.

Larry smiled. "No, sweetie. There's nothing to worry—"

The glass above them shattered as something came hurtling through the window. Moments later, white smoke quickly filled the room.

Crystal let out an ear-piercing scream.

CHAPTER 2

Samantha groaned. "I'm not sure I'm up for a camping trip. The cold, the damp air, sleeping the ground, none of it sounds appealing."

Kathy held the steering wheel loosely as she drove into the Allegheny National Forest. "It's only for a few days."

"Yeah, which is the longest I've ever gone away from Josh."

"Sam, we need this weekend to be just the two of us as sisters. Ever since I moved back in, we've done nothing but bicker with each other."

Samantha shrugged and looked out the window at the pine trees passing by them. "That's true. But with the rain we've been having and the temperature dropping, I'm not sure I'm really in the mood to camp."

"I'm *never* in the mood to camp," Kathy said. "Trust me. I hate it. This girl needs a warm, soft bed to sleep in each night and a hot shower to greet her in the morning. But judging from the flyer I picked up at the Chamber of Commerce, this place looks more like…remote living than traditional camping."

"*Remote living*?" Samantha asked.

"It has most of the comforts of home, but in a remote location."

"Hot water?"

"Got it."

"Electricity?"

"That too."

"Beds?"

"Twin size bunk beds, but they seemed to be nice and plump from the pictures. *And*, they have a fireplace, so that'll be nice."

Samantha couldn't deny that. She loved her fireplace back home and wished that there was one up in her and Steven's bedroom. But by the time the second story was added, technological advances didn't require a fireplace in each room. "Okay, what about a kitchen?"

"It's a kitchenette, but it has a stove burner, a sink, and a small fridge," Kathy said. "Everything we need, just…smaller."

"I hope you're right about this place." Samantha had been so busy at work and with Josh that she hadn't really been involved in the plans for this little girls' trip that Kathy had insisted on.

Of course, a part of her just didn't want to go on it at all, so subconsciously she had been avoiding planning it hoping that it would never come. Alas, that method had failed.

"Sam, we're going to have a good time," Kathy said. "We'll relax. Unwind. Talk. Play some cards. It'll be fun. It's been a while since it's been just the two of us."

"I know. It will be fun. But I'm a mother now, I can't *not* think about my kid."

"I get that, but I want you to focus on what we're going to do on this trip," Kathy countered. "Hiking, relaxing by the fire, listening to the wind blow the leaves, reading. You'll come back from this trip a whole new person."

"But I already miss him."

"I know, but he's in good hands. Steven is his father. He is more than capable of taking care of Josh. Plus, it's not like Josh is a tiny infant anymore. He's ten months old!"

It was hard to believe that Samantha's little baby boy was already past several of his first milestones and was quickly growing into a little toddler. It seemed like she had just been in the hospital giving birth. But then, she figured she'd probably be thinking that for the rest of his life. She felt as if she couldn't squeeze him enough, hold him enough, love him enough. And the thought of spending more time away from him than she had to was heart-wrenching.

"There's a turn up here, but I don't remember which one to take." Kathy squinted as she looked for the road signs along the curving road. "Check the map."

From the floor in front of her, Samantha pulled up the map and spread it out in her lap. "What road are we on now?"

"Route 666."

Samantha raised her eyebrows as she studied the map. "That seems like a bad sign."

"Oh, come on. It's just a route number. Stop trying to ruin this weekend already and just enjoy it. We just past Pierson Hill Road. I'm looking for Bobb's Creek Road. I know it's on the left, but how far up is it?"

"Um…not much farther, I don't think."

"How much is 'not much farther'?"

"Uh…I don't know. I think I lost track of where we are." Samantha turned the map, but none of it was making any sense. It didn't help that there were very few landmarks and so many twists and turns in the road.

"Here's a gas station," Kathy said. "I'll fill up and you go in and ask for directions." She pulled off the road to a single-pump station. An attendant stood out by the pump to fill up the car.

Once the car stopped, Samantha got out and walked to the tiny convenience store. Taped to the glass door were several missing persons postings. One for a man named Rick Gallagher and the other for Clay Clark. Both postings had pictures of men who were only about five or so years older than Samantha and Kathy themselves.

Samantha shook her head. It was a shame when any two

people, but especially two *young* people just up and disappeared. But what stood out to her was that they were both men. And, judging by the looks of them, they were men who looked like they could take care of themselves. The fact that they had gone missing spoke of something else.

But Samantha didn't want to think about that.

She opened the door and tried to put it out of her mind, but she couldn't help but feel the sense of dread that something terrible was coming. There were so many signs: Route 666, the missing persons, Samantha's unease with the trip from the very beginning.

Then again, she and Kathy had faced worse things than anything that could possibly be lurking in the woods. What she was feeling was probably a mixture of parent guilt and sister guilt. Being trapped between a rock and a hard place. She couldn't spend all her time with her son and ignore her sister. And she couldn't spend alone time with her sister without being away from her son.

"Can I help you?" the store clerk asked when she walked up to the counter. He was a late-middle-aged man with salt-and-pepper hair and a completely gray mustache. He wore a flannel shirt and jeans. Wedged between two of his fingers, a cigarette burned in his hand.

"Hi, my sister and I are camping out here and we got turned around," Samantha said. "Would you be able to help point me in the right direction?"

The man took a puff of his cigarette, then smiled and let the smoke slip out of his mouth. "Sure thing, madam! Lay that map right here and let's see if we can't get you to where you're looking to go."

Samantha set the map down and pointed to a particular route running through the forest. "We're here, right?"

"No, ma'am." He pointed to another spot further down on the same route. "We're all the way down here. Where is it you're heading to?"

"Shady Acres."

The man sat back, surprise on his face. "The Fisher property?"

Samantha pulled out the flyer from her back pocket. Sure enough, on the back it said that Shady Acres was owned by the Fisher family. "I guess so."

"Are you sure you want to go there?" He raised his eyebrows as he looked at her.

"Uh…well…" Samantha hesitated, her fears about this weekend on high alert. "I mean, we've already paid for a cabin, so yes, we do."

He took another puff of his cigarette and nodded slowly. "Okay then. Just be careful out there. Now, here's what you need to do. Keep going down this route, then you'll want to turn left onto Bobb's Creek Road. It's hidden in the trees. Dirt road, drive slow, make sure you put it in low gear because the inclines out here can be murder on your engine. Now, the Fisher property will be on your right once you turn onto Bobb's Creek. It's at the top of a hill. The driveway's hidden. Not many people go down there, so you'll have to keep your eyes open for it."

Samantha nodded. "Got it. Thanks."

"You said it was you and your sister who were staying there?"

"Yeah."

"You don't have any boyfriends or anyone else staying with you?"

"My husband's back at home with our son." She felt her heart rate begin to pick up. "Why?"

He shrugged and averted his eyes. "Just curious. Be careful out there."

Samantha forced a smile. "Thanks for the tip—and the directions. I appreciate it."

She turned and left the convenience store, trying her best not to worry about the encounter she had just had.

"Ready?" Kathy asked back at the car.

"Yep." As Samantha climbed back in, she considered telling Kathy about her conversation with the helpful store clerk—or the missing persons postings—but she didn't. As the older sibling, and the one who was already having reservations about this trip, she decided to take on the burden of worry all on her own.

Using the directions Samantha had been given, they found their way to Shady Acres without a problem. The tip the clerk had offered about low gear helped Kathy navigate the car up the steep incline on the gravel road without the tires spinning out or the engine overexerting itself.

"He said it would be hidden," Samantha said as she studied the passing greenery for any signs or break in the overgrowth. "There!"

Kathy hit the brakes—perhaps harder than she needed to—and pivoted the car down a gravel driveway. Branches scraped the side of the car as they passed through a particularly tight spot in the brush before opening up to a clearing with a wide driveway where there were two trucks parked. To the right side of the driveway was a two-story barn and to the left was a ramshackle house.

Based on the crude map on the back of the flyer from the Chamber of Commerce, that was the "main house." Samantha had envisioned something more regal or stately. Instead, the house looked tired. Paint had chipped off the siding, other spots had dry rotted wood, and the roof looked a little worse for wear. Beside it sat several rusted cars in the weeds. Over the hum of the engine, they heard dogs barking from somewhere that Samantha couldn't place.

But through the front door on the porch, the warm glow of light came through and the house looked warm and inviting inside. Maybe, Samantha figured, she shouldn't judge a book by its cover.

"*This* is it?" Kathy asked, looking at the house.

"Yeah." Samantha pointed to the sign at the front of the driveway that said "Shady Acres." It looked identical to the one on the flyer. "And over there is probably where the road to the cabins are." She pointed to the driveway that passed right by the barn. It was filled with muddy potholes, but was very clearly meant for vehicles.

"Oh. The trees over there look nice with the colors," Kathy said. "Maybe the cabins are really nice too."

Samantha reached for her sister's arm before she could exit. "Are you sure you want to stay here? We could change our minds. It was only a two-hour drive."

"Yes, I'm sure. And I'm exhausted from the drive. Plus, we've already paid, so let's just go check it out." Kathy pulled her arm free from her sister's grasp, but paused before opening the door, her eyes locked on the house. "It does look kind of creepy, though, doesn't it?"

Samantha nodded.

"We're just being paranoid. We'll be fine." Kathy looked back at Samantha and smiled. "Besides, we're witches. They can't hold a candle to us."

"Famous last words," Samantha grumbled as she climbed out of the car as well.

The two sisters walked up to the front porch, neither of them having a good feeling about their lodgings.

CHAPTER 3

- 1980 -

Even from his room at the end of his family's trailer, fifteen-year-old Donovan Fisher could hear his parents arguing. It was always the same things that spawned the arguments: suspected infidelity, insecurities, laziness. Their constant arguing was why Donovan had decided that he was never getting married. It just seemed like a waste. Two people who lived together, relied on each other to survive, but couldn't stand each other?

No, Donovan would learn how to be self-sufficient so he wouldn't ever have to rely on anyone else.

Of course, his parents weren't the only example of a married couple that Donovan was exposed to. There was also his Uncle Jim and Aunt Sue, who owned the property

Donovan and his parents lived on.

Uncle Jim and Aunt Sue seemed like a solid couple. *That* was the type of marriage Donovan could see having someday. But how often did a good marriage like theirs happen? Uncle Jim and Aunt Sue's marriage worked because both were self-sufficient. At least, Uncle Jim was. He owned his land, hunted his land, and rented out even more land closer to the city for farmers to farm on. He provided for his family without ever having to leave home. Meanwhile, Aunt Sue stayed back at the house, cooked up the food that was farmed on their land, and kept up with everything else on the homestead. They were a team.

"You're always eyeing her up!" Donovan's mother, Gretchen, shouted across the small trailer. "Every time we go in there, you're suddenly all softy and, 'Oh, is there anything I can help you with to make your shift a little easier?'" Donovan heard a gagging sound and then, "It's *disgusting*! And embarrassing. I seen the way you been looking at her!"

"I ain't looking at no one!" Rodney, Donovan's father, shouted back. "Besides, is it a crime to offer a little help? It's not like I'm pressing myself up against her and playing dumb like you do to them guys at the bar!"

"It's called flirting for bigger tips, Rod! If I didn't do that, we wouldn't be able to afford this piece of shit we live in! Don't think your whore at the gas station can afford nothing more than this!"

"There's nothing going on! Would you drop it?"

"No, because I know you been lying through them teeth! You come up with every excuse in the book to go see her! Are you screwing her? Tell me, so I know whether I'm going to catch any diseases from that slut."

"Can't catch nothing when we ain't sleeping together!"

Donovan had heard enough. He wanted out, but the only way out was through the only door in the trailer. If he made a quick exit while they were arguing, maybe they wouldn't even notice.

He opened the door and paused to see what kind of reaction he'd get from his parents. When they paid him no mind, he walked quickly to the door, but as he put his hand on the handle, his mother's voice rose.

"And where the hell do you think *you're* going, Don?"

He turned and kept one hand on the doorknob. "Going over to Uncle Jim's for a bit."

"Oh." Her tone softened a little. "Well, don't stay over there too long. I want to see you before I head off to work."

Rodney snorted. "Yeah. Your mother needs to get all gussied up so some stranger can put his hands on her."

"I told you, that's for *tips*!"

"If that was true, we wouldn't be living on my brother's property."

"That's because you can't get off your ass and find a—"

Donovan made his escape while they were distracted. Once

outside, he went right behind the trailer and into the thick of the woods.

Uncle Jim said he liked to keep his property in the Allegheny Mountains as natural as possible to encourage the wildlife to settle there so they could hunt and provide for the family. So there was no set trail, other than the ones the deer had made themselves.

As far back as Donovan could remember, Uncle Jim had always been bringing them extra venison or turkey meat that he got while hunting. He loved hunting and had even begun teaching Donovan how to do it properly. Everything from what to wear, what to look for, and what different animals were attracted to, to preparing the meat for eating and how to cook it for best the best taste. Uncle Jim knew everything and Donovan was like a sponge, absorbing it all eagerly.

By the time Donovan reached Uncle Jim's house, he saw his cousins, Pete and Kurt, out back with Uncle Jim target-practicing with their rifles. Donovan's shoulders sunk a little at the sight, but still he went up to greet them.

Donovan didn't have his own gun. Sure, Uncle Jim let him borrow his whenever, but he didn't have his own to practice at home. And the one time he had asked his parents for one, Donovan's father laughed in his face and told him how they could barely afford food and cigarettes, so why in the hell would they buy him a gun?

"Mind if I jump in?" Donovan asked his cousins in

greeting. "When you're done."

Pete and Kurt both nodded at him, then returned to aiming their rifles.

Donovan sat on a nearby stack of pallets and swung his feet under him, trying not to look too pathetic. Sure, this was better than listening to his parents argue, but he still didn't quite feel like he fit in.

"Donovan!" Uncle Jim's voice boomed across the yard.

He turned and saw his uncle waving him toward the barn. He jumped down and hurried across the yard to join his uncle.

"How you been, son?"

"I'm okay," Donovan said. "Mom and Dad are fighting again, so I thought I'd come over here."

Uncle Jim let out a heavy sigh, then reached for a rifle from his work bench. It was a new one, Donovan recognized that much. He had a slight fascination with firearms. Perhaps because he wasn't allowed to own one. Or maybe it was because Uncle Jim and Pete and Kurt all had one of their own.

"I have a surprise for you," Uncle Jim said. "But you can't tell your parents about it—especially your father. Understand? I don't want him to feel emasculated or nothing."

Donovan nodded. He wasn't *quite* sure what *emasculated* meant, but he knew it was bad.

"Here's your very own .22."

Donovan hesitantly reached for it with wide eyes. "Seriously?"

Human

Uncle Jim smiled. "You've earned it, son. Now get out there and target practice along with your cousins. You're going to need it."

FIND ALL THE BOOKS IN THE COVEN SERIES!

More by the Author

To find more books by the author, visit
DavidNethBooks.com/Books

* * *

Subscribe to his newsletter to be the first to know of new
releases and special deals!
DavidNethBooks.com/Newsletter

* * *

**If you enjoyed the book, please consider leaving a
review on Goodreads or the retailer you bought it from.**
Reviews help potential readers determine whether
they'll enjoy a book, so any comments on what you
thought of the story would be very helpful!

About the Author

David Neth is the author of the Coven series, the Under the Moon series, Heat series, the Fuse series, and other stories. He lives in Batavia, NY, where he dreams of a successful publishing career and opening his own bookstore.

Also writes small town romance as D. Allen.

www.DavidNethBooks.com

www.facebook.com/DavidNethBooks